Dancing Under the Mistletoe

A Victorian Romance Novella

Book IV of
The Seven Curses of London Series

Lana Williams
USA Today Bestselling Author

TRUSTING THE WOLFE, a Novella, Book .5
LOVING THE HAWKE, Book 1
CHARMING THE SCHOLAR, Book 2
RESCUING THE EARL, Book 3
DANCING UNDER THE MISTLETOE, Book 4, a Novella
TEMPTING THE SCOUNDREL, Book 5, a Novella
ROMANCING THE ROGUE, A Regency Prequel
FALLING FOR THE VISCOUNT, Book 6
DARING THE DUKE, Book 7
WISHING UPON A CHRISTMAS STAR, a Novella, Book 8
RUBY'S GAMBLE, a Novella
GAMBLING FOR THE GOVERNESS, Book 9
REEMING THE LADY, Book 10

Want to make sure you know when my next book is released? Sign up for my newsletter on my website at www.lanawilliams.net.

Dedication

To all the readers out there who love the Christmas season and believe in the magic it holds all year round. Merry Christmas!

Chapter One

London, England, December 1870

Katherine Flemming breathed a sigh of relief as the train pulled away from the station, its whistle blowing a forlorn farewell to the bustling city.

Farewell to Miss Flitchard, another identity she had now set aside.

Farewell to her life, once again.

She closed her eyes, wondering how many more times she'd need to run...to start over. How many more times she'd have the strength of will to do so. Swallowing back the lump in her throat, she opened her eyes to study the other travelers in the crowded compartment, if only to reassure herself she wasn't being followed.

At least not yet. For now she was safe.

He would find her eventually. He always did.

"Are ye visitin' family for the holiday?" the cheerful woman sitting beside her asked. A smile lit her face, her warm brown eyes shifting between the two young children between her and Katherine.

"A friend." Although Katherine still had a difficult time believing she should call Grace Hawke a friend, as she was the Countess of Adair. Perhaps it had been a mistake to accept the invitation to spend the holidays at the Adairs' country estate in Northamptonshire, but she didn't know where else to go. Her options were narrowing each time she had to start over.

"Oh, that's lovely. Nothin' like spendin' time with friends or family over Christmas."

The woman chattered on, sharing her holiday plans. Katherine only caught part of what she said, as her thoughts lingered on her abrupt departure from the dressmaker's shop where she'd worked for the past six months. No doubt Mrs. Danby, the owner, was cursing her name—or at least the name she'd assumed this time—for leaving without notice.

Yet Katherine had no choice. Not when one of the girls who worked in the shop next door told her a man was asking questions about her.

When her fellow traveler's attention shifted to her children, Katherine retrieved the embossed invitation from her satchel to read it once again. She'd been stunned when it had been delivered to her one-room flat by a liveried footman, complete with a train ticket.

After much pondering, Katherine surmised that Grace had sent the invitation with the hope that Katherine might assist her with the new wardrobe she'd purchased from Mrs. Danby. After all, it wouldn't do for a recently married countess to dress in half-mourning when her new husband was alive and well. Katherine quelled the pang of envy at the memory of the joy on Grace's face as she planned her hastily arranged wedding. Apparently it had been important for the earl to marry prior to his birthday, and Grace had been more than happy to oblige.

Katherine knew she didn't belong at the house party any more than she belonged serving as a seamstress's assistant. Somewhere in the past five years of slipping from one identity to another, she'd lost herself.

There was no chance of finding her true self at a Christmas celebration given by an earl and countess, but it would provide her with a fortnight to create a new identity. The invitation had arrived at the perfect time. Katherine had exchanged the first-class train ticket for one in second class and pocketed the money with only a sliver of guilt. Grace wouldn't begrudge her if she knew. But Katherine didn't intend to tell her. It would be one more secret added to her growing pile.

No one truly knew her or her past. Except him.

She was normally careful to avoid connections with others, but somehow Grace had slipped through her defenses. Perhaps that was because of the lady's uncertainty when they'd first met at the dressmaker's, as though no longer sure of her own tastes and opinions. Katherine hadn't been able to resist encouraging her. Watching Grace bloom over the past months had been a true pleasure—one of the few in Katherine's life. The love Grace had found with her earl made Katherine sigh with both envy and delight. She had yet to meet the man who'd swept Grace off her feet, but by the end of this day, she supposed that would change.

Her stomach lurched at the thought. Meeting new people brought a certain risk. There was always a chance they might recognize her or know her past. If so, her holiday would end before it began.

The sprawl of London and its soot-filled fog gave way to rolling hills and stubbled fields as the train continued its journey north. They stopped frequently as the day passed. Somehow the lack of buildings and people made Katherine uneasy. She was a city girl and had never ventured far from London. Northamptonshire might as well have been in another country as far as she was concerned.

"Did ye bring yer lunch?" Nancy, the woman next to her, asked. At Katherine's denial, she held out a basket. "We have plenty, and you must be hungry."

"Thank you." Katherine gratefully accepted an apple after making certain the children had all they wanted. In her haste to leave, she hadn't thought to bring anything.

Frost formed on the train windows as the afternoon waned, much to the delight of the children, who stood to draw patterns in it. Katherine stared at the perfect crystals, a sign that winter was nearly upon them. The cold weather complicated her existence, especially when she no longer had a place to live.

She traced a frosted crystal, amazed at the intricacy of it, the beauty. Her hope for Christmas was simple—find a new place, a new identity, until he took it from her. Again.

And a snowflake.

That was her second wish. She wanted to see one perfect snowflake fall from the sky. If she did, she'd take that as a sign that all would be well. At least for the holidays.

With a past she wanted to forget, a future she couldn't have, one day at a time was the best she could hope for.

Cole Dumont flipped up the collar of his wool coat to keep the chill from chasing down his neck then flicked the reins of the horses. How he'd been talked into this errand was still unclear.

Yet anything was better than watching the Earl of Adair and his new countess, Lady Adair, as they prepared Crawford House for Christmas festivities. Every servant in the large mansion had been running to and fro with piles of greenery and decorations for the holiday celebration. The happiness of the newly married couple was both touching and annoying.

Cole's own home stood only a few miles away, empty and dark—just as he preferred it.

But remaining there during the holiday with all the family traditions brought too many memories, too much pain.

He'd easily tossed aside the invitation to join the Adairs' for a fortnight of celebrations when it had arrived. The very idea had given him the shivers. Two weeks of conversing and celebrating Christmas sounded like his version of hell.

But as the weather grew colder and the scents and sights of the season filtered their way into his tenants' homes and the village, his mood had turned darker and darker.

He'd thought this year would be easier, but as November folded into December, he realized time had not eased anything.

After pacing the quiet halls of his home, he'd known he couldn't stay there. Not until Christmas was over.

As a baron with just one holding, Cole hadn't expected to have anything in common with Adair, but after meeting him several times over the years, Cole found he admired the man. They shared a love of the land and took pleasure in seeing what they could do to help the people who lived here. Neither felt the need to talk beyond the basic necessities.

Cole hoped to convince Adair to sell him one of his prize mares as well. Surely a new wife and a holiday party would put the earl in a generous mood. If Cole focused, he could pretend that was the reason he'd agreed to stay at Crawford House over the holidays rather than his own issues.

The village came into sight, draped in greenery and other décor. The scents of gingerbread and cinnamon lingered in the air along with wood smoke.

He ran a gloved hand over his nose to chase away the smells.

He greeted several familiar faces with a wave or a tip of his top hat as he passed through the village, heading toward the train station at the opposite end. This place had been his home his entire life. He'd ventured far away for brief periods of time, but always returned. He closed his eyes briefly as a wave of regret and guilt rolled over him, nearly crushing him with its weight. Because the last time he'd left, he'd returned too late.

As he arrived at the station, the train pulled into view, its whistle sounding mournful in the dusky light. Or perhaps it was just he who felt melancholy. As long as his mood didn't deteriorate beyond that into despair. He drew a deep breath of the brisk air to chase away the shadows and found a place to wait with the phaeton until the passengers disembarked.

Countess Adair—or Grace, as she insisted he call her—had given a vague description of a slim woman in her twenties with dark hair and spectacles. He wasn't certain that was enough for him to recognize her, but surely the woman would be looking for someone to pick her up.

"Good evening, Lord Barclay."

Cole turned to find Terrance Penney, the blacksmith, drawing near. "Done for the day?"

"Indeed. Headed home for supper with the family." Penney cringed, as he glanced up at Cole as though realizing his mistake too late.

Smothering a sigh, Cole only nodded as he

glanced at the passengers now filling the platform. Weary of the looks of pity he garnered each day, he wished people would forget his loss. Perhaps that would allow him to do so as well.

Not that he wanted to forget his family...only the aching loss of them.

Realizing he made no sense, even in his own head, he nodded. "Give Mrs. Penney my best. Are your sons and their families joining you for the holiday?"

The man's eyes lit up. "They'll be here at the end of the week."

Another glance at the platform showed the crowd had thinned, leaving only a few who fit the description of his target.

"I believe the person I'm to meet has arrived. Enjoy your time with them." He secured the reins and, with a final nod to Penney, hopped down and made his way to the platform. The tidy, modestly dressed woman standing by herself didn't wear spectacles, but no one else matched his instructions. "Miss Flitchard?"

The lady he addressed was looking in the opposite direction and didn't respond to his inquiry. Either she wasn't Grace's friend or she had difficulty hearing.

The woman seemed to at last realize she'd been spoken to and turned to him. "I'm sorry?"

"Miss Katherine Flitchard?" Cole asked.

"Yes. Of course." She blinked up at him, her dark eyes appearing startled in the dusky light. Her cheeks were pink from the frosty air along with the tip of her upturned nose. A brown hat perched upon her head, matching her woolen cloak. "I'm Miss Flitchard."

"I was asked to collect you."

"How thoughtful of you." She studied him as though determining whether to believe him. "And you are?"

"Cole Dumont, at your service." He gave a bow, not bothering to share his title. This was the country, after all, not London. A glance at the ground near her practical leather boots showed two well-worn bags.

As he reached for them, she asked, "Who asked you to collect me?"

He paused, frowning at her. "The Countess of Adair." He wasn't certain what answer she was looking for. Was she concerned he was some nefarious man sent to abduct her rather than deliver her to the Adairs' country estate? "I'm to take you to Crawford House."

"What's the countess's first name?"

He paused before answering, surprised at her caution. "Grace."

"Very well." Seeming satisfied he was who he said he was, she gave a nod. A single dip of her slightly tilted head.

Why that simple gesture caught his interest, he didn't know. She raised a brow as he continued to study her.

"I thought you wore spectacles." Surely her delicate features, those dark, winged brows, and the long, curved sweep of her lashes wouldn't be quite so appealing if she had them on.

"Oh." She looked down at her purse and patted it. "I do, but I kept them in my bag during the trip. I mainly wear them to see up close."

A deeper shade of rose bloomed in her cheeks, whether from him staring or from his far too personal question, he didn't know. He dragged his gaze away, looking anywhere but at her. "No matter. Is this all your luggage then?"

"There's also a crate." She glanced over her shoulder to a large wooden box nearby.

"Brought quite a few clothes with you, did you?" Cole was astonished at the size of the thing.

"Oh, that's not mine." At his frown, she gestured to the crate. "Or rather, it is in my care, but it's for the countess. She ordered several gowns before leaving London."

"I see." He looked at the phaeton, well aware it wouldn't fit. "I'll arrange to have it delivered."

"I'm her seamstress. That's why I'm here. To see her gowns safely arrived."

Cole frowned at her, wondering at her explanation. "Countess Adair only mentioned that you were her friend."

There was no mistaking the surprise that crossed her features. Why would she be surprised to hear that? Surely she knew whether or not they were friends.

He dismissed his curiosity and called for a porter to deliver the crate later. Soon enough, Miss Flitchard was seated beside him, and they were driving through the village toward Crawford House.

"Oh, my," she whispered reverently.

He turned to see her studying the shops along the street, the warm glow of light visible in many of the windows. Several people hurried past, intent on finishing their business before the shops closed for the evening.

She glanced at him as though feeling his regard. "It's quite...picturesque, isn't it?"

He tried to see the village through her eyes. He'd done his best to ignore the decorations, but could see why she might find the village appealing, especially this time of year.

She cleared her throat as though self-conscious. "London is much different."

"Indeed it is." He watched from the corner of his eye, unable to dismiss her as easily as he'd expected.

"How long of a drive is it?"

"Not far. Are you warm enough?"

"Yes, thank you." But the shiver that passed through her belied her words.

"There's a fur cover under the seat, if you'd like." For a moment, he thought she'd refuse, but then she retrieved it and spread it over both their laps.

His breath caught as she leaned close, her kind gesture catching him off guard. It had been a long time since anyone had made an effort to care for his wellbeing. He had no idea how to react.

"How's that?" she asked, looking up at him as she

straightened the cover over him, her gloved fingers touching his thigh.

The waning evening light cast a spell over him as he looked into her eyes. She was close enough now that he could feel her body heat, could see the small scar just below the outer corner of her eye. He had the oddest urge to trace it with his finger and ask what caused it, to connect with her on some level.

But that would never do. He broke eye contact and eased back, not wanting to be rude but needing to keep his distance. His sanity depended on it. Forming a relationship was not in his plans. It was too risky of an endeavor and wouldn't end well.

He flicked the reins and focused on the road ahead. This woman was a stranger briefly passing through his life. Nothing more. He'd do well to remember that.

Chapter Two

Katherine spent enough time observing others to realize that her friendly overture had been firmly rejected. She couldn't help the hurt that speared through her as he eased away and focused on the road.

Silly of her to care. After all, he was a stranger.

No doubt he was married with children and thought her overly forward. She was not here to form friendships, but to assist Grace with her new gowns. With a quiet sigh she kept all to herself, she pulled her wool cloak tighter and glanced about.

The quaint village gave way to open fields, with hints of civilization becoming fewer and fewer. Evening had fallen in full, leaving the sky an inky black covered with pinpoints of light. She'd never seen anything like it before. In London, only a few stars were visible at night. Nothing like this. The longer she looked, the more lights appeared. It reminded her of a pattern full of pinpricks, held up to the window at the modiste's.

"My goodness." As soon as the words escaped her lips, she wished she could take them back. Surely he thought her awe at the sight silly.

Rather than scoff at her in derision, he looked up as though trying to see what she did. "It's a sight, isn't it? I forget that you can't see many stars when in the city."

Her gaze lingered on the strong column of his throat, the line of his jaw, the shadow of his whiskers, before studying the night sky again. He was a very attractive man. "It makes me feel rather insignificant."

His dark eyes caught hers, his surprised expression just visible in the lantern light. "It does, doesn't it?"

She bit her lower lip, determined not to say anything more, else he'd think her ridiculous. Instead she looked up again, wondering why the sight of all those stars put such a lump in her throat.

It had been a long, tiring day, she reminded herself. How remiss of her not to respond when he'd called her name at the train station, but sometimes she forgot what name she was using, just as she'd forgotten to wear her spectacles.

She'd have some work ahead of her when she arrived, as Grace would want to have one or two of her gowns fitted. That would make her day longer yet.

She should've thought to see if any food was available for purchase at the train station. Or maybe once everyone retired for the evening, she might sneak down to the kitchen and see if the cook would provide something for her. Her stomach grumbled as though protesting the possible delay of an evening meal. Thinking of food was obviously a mistake.

"Hungry, are you? I am as well." He shared a small smile that eased the coolness she'd felt from him earlier. "No doubt they'll have supper waiting for us upon our arrival."

She didn't bother to correct him. While that might be true for him, she wasn't truly a guest. "The cold air always seems to bring out my appetite, not to mention the upcoming holiday festivities."

The glimmer of friendliness she'd seen in his expression vanished at the mention of holidays. He must not enjoy them. Some people didn't. She had fond memories of Christmas as a child but had spent the past few years alone.

Katherine hoped to have a few moments to enjoy the Christmas season. The notion of spending some of it with Grace provided a sense of anticipation she hadn't experienced for a long time.

Something about this time of year used to give her renewed hope. Unfortunately, the small bud of it had been stolen, and she wasn't certain if she could get it back.

Adair handed Cole a glass of brandy in the library upon his return. "We appreciate you helping us by retrieving Miss Flitchard."

"Happy to be of assistance." Cole took a long draught of the golden liquid, appreciating the burn of it down his throat into his chest. The warm sensation in his body felt odd—as though the sudden heat shocked the part of him that was always so cold.

Adair leveled a look at him. "I was pleasantly surprised you accepted our invitation to stay with us over the holidays."

Cole clenched his jaw, not wanting to offer too much of an explanation. Speaking of his entire family dying—mother, father, and sister—never made him feel better. Not that he wanted to forget them. Far from it. He only wanted to put the pain of their death behind him. Though thus far, that had been an elusive wish.

Since Adair patiently waited, Cole finally said, "I prefer to stay busy during the holidays."

"I'm terribly sorry. Losing your family just before Christmas must've been incredibly painful. How long has it been?"

"Two years." He swirled the liquid in his glass, keeping his gaze focused on that rather than meeting the sympathy in Adair's. How he hated the pity directed his way. Why didn't people realize that only made it worse?

"We're pleased you're here." As though sensing Cole would prefer to change the subject, Adair continued, "How did you find Miss Flitchard? I have yet to meet her, though Grace speaks highly of her."

Cole glanced up, relieved at the change of subject. "She seems quite..." He hesitated, surprised that the first word that came to mind was *beautiful*. Watching her expression as she stared up at the night sky had been a delight. But the last thing he wanted to do was suggest he was attracted to the woman. "Pleasant. I don't believe she's spent much time in the country."

"A city girl, eh? Well, we'll have to hope she comes to appreciate the many advantages the countryside has to offer."

Cole nodded, thinking she'd already found something to admire about their corner of the world. Not that it should matter to him what she thought.

"And how are you finding married life?" Cole asked.

Adair's grin said it all. He touched his cheek, as though his smile felt unfamiliar. "I never thought such happiness was possible."

Cole returned his smile, appreciating Adair's joy. "Here's to many more years of marital bliss." He raised his glass, ignoring the twinge of envy that filled him. In his experience, the higher a person's joy, the further they fell when it was ripped away. Such joy was not worth the risk. Of that he had no doubt.

Katherine looked about the luxurious bedroom, certain there must be some sort of mistake. She peeked out the door, but the maid who'd shown her to the room was gone.

She turned back to the room to stare at the inviting four-poster bed with its warm brown and gold covers. Different shades of the same colors were used throughout the large room, giving the room a cozy, welcoming feel. A fire burned brightly with inviting chairs before it, and Katherine found herself moving toward the warm glow.

Surely this bedroom was not for the seamstress sent to accompany the new wardrobe, even if the gowns were for a countess. Yet Katherine's two well-worn bags sat on the floor before the bureau.

A quiet knock on the door interrupted Katherine's musings. Before she could respond, the door opened and Grace entered.

"I am so thrilled you're here," Grace exclaimed, her smile bright and welcoming, as she came forward to embrace her.

Her delight took Katherine by surprise, but she returned the hug all the same. Grace's affection created a warm, fuzzy feeling inside her. How long had it been since someone greeted her thusly?

She blinked back tears at the thought. Neither Grace's welcome nor the holidays were any reason to suddenly become maudlin. That would never do.

"Thank you for inviting me. Mr. Dumont didn't have room for the crate containing your gowns, but the porter reassured us it would be delivered promptly."

"You mean Lord Barclay? That's so like him not to mention his title. Isn't he nice?" Before Katherine could respond, Grace continued, "You brought the new gowns with you? You didn't need to do that. I hope it didn't complicate your travel here."

Katherine frowned, confused at Grace's words. "Of course, I did. Didn't you want them here? And

I'm afraid the maid delivered me to the wrong room." She swept her hand through the air toward the fine furnishings.

Grace looked about. "Don't you like this one? It's one of my favorites, which is why I selected it for you. But we can move you to another if you prefer."

Katherine stared at Grace. "It's not very practical for a seamstress. Wouldn't you rather I took a room closer to the servants?"

"You are here as our guest, as my friend. Not for your wonderful skills with a needle and thread." Grace studied her, making Katherine uncomfortable, as it felt as if she was seeing far more than Katherine would like. "Is all well? You look rather tired."

"I—I left the city rather abruptly. Mrs. Danby wasn't pleased." Katherine glanced away, hoping Grace would accept that as explanation enough.

"You left your position?" Grace reached for her hands and held them tight.

"Yes." Grace's affection and support caused the lump in her throat to return.

"Good. I don't care for that woman. You'll be far better off doing something else. In the meantime, you'll stay with us and rest and relax."

"Oh, but I couldn't."

Grace tilted her head, her gaze sweeping over Katherine once more. "You're overdue for a few days off, and what better time for that than the holidays? Besides, I'm going to need your assistance. We are having several guests and have only just arrived at Crawford House ourselves. I can't possibly get everything done that I need to."

Katherine's unease faded. Somehow, knowing she had a purpose here relaxed her. "I'm happy to help in whatever capacity you need."

"Excellent. I didn't want Cole—Lord Barclay—to feel out of place, so one of your tasks is to befriend him."

Katherine's unease flew back in full force, especially when she thought of his attractive features, the strength of him, the sizzle of awareness that filled her the entire ride from the train station. Not to mention that she now knew he was a titled lord. "Oh, I couldn't."

"Why?"

Katherine blinked, her mind blank. *Because I am attracted to him*? That would never do. *Because he's a lord*? That seemed better. "He wouldn't want to spend time with a seamstress."

"I hardly think your position at a dressmaker's shop defines who you are, nor will it matter to him."

Katherine clenched her fists as panic filled her. Without that, she wasn't anyone. Or no one she recognized. She immersed herself in whatever position she took, in whatever identity she invented. At this moment, she was between those things, leaving her rudderless.

"Katherine." Grace ran her hands up and down Katherine's arms. "I am so glad you're here. As my friend. As a guest in my home. I promise the festivities will be great fun, and you'll enjoy our friends."

"I can't." As hurt filled Grace's expression and her

hands dropped away, Katherine reached for her. "I mean, I value your friendship more than I can say. But I don't belong at the house party of a countess." She shook her head, the idea of playing such a role frightening her. "I certainly don't have the proper clothes for such a task."

Grace's smile returned. "Then it's a good thing we're nearly the same size, isn't it? Don't worry about any of that. This is my first Christmas with Tristan. Matthew is excited and so am I. I want everything to be perfect, and having you here makes it so. Nothing else matters."

Katherine could only nod. She had yet to meet Grace's son, Matthew, or her husband. What else could she possibly say?

"Let us join the men for supper. I'm starving." Grace looped her arm through Katherine's to pull her from the room toward the stairs. "You need only relax and enjoy yourself. And might I remind you that miracles happen during the holiday season. Who knows what might happen with a little Christmas magic?"

Miracles? Magic? Katherine could only shake her head. Such words were not in her vocabulary. *Survival* was a much more familiar term.

Yet as she and Grace descended the stairs, Grace's enthusiasm became contagious as she shared her plans for the holiday celebration. While Katherine had no intention of setting aside her goal of determining a new place to live and a new identity, perhaps she could still enjoy a reprieve from her normal life. Hadn't she wanted a few moments to enjoy Christmas? This might be her chance.

She couldn't help but think of the shadows she'd seen in Lord Barclay's eyes as they'd entered the festively decorated foyer of Crawford House. Perhaps she could find a way to help chase away those, however briefly.

Chapter Three

Cole settled into his breakfast, grateful for the unexpected solitude of the early morning for a few precious minutes. It was too soon to be so optimistic that he might be the only early riser, as most of the guests had yet to arrive. That didn't mean he couldn't hope.

Solitude was normally his constant companion, and one he appreciated. But during the holidays, it became something else entirely—a demon he had to fight, else be dragged into the depths of despair.

He shook his head at his musings. Rarely was he given to drama, nor did he appreciate it in others. Somehow the Christmas season made him more vulnerable to it. Miss Flitchard didn't seem the type to indulge in drama either. She seemed a rather practical soul.

Not that he knew her well. One phaeton ride and some bonding over a starry night sky didn't make them friends. Yet he couldn't deny that connection he'd felt with her, however briefly.

His eggs and sausage were perfectly done, still hot. He nodded his thanks at the attentive footman, who refilled his coffee before easing back to blend into the wallpaper.

A form appeared in Cole's peripheral vision, and he glanced up to see Miss Flitchard hesitating in the doorway. Maybe he wasn't the only guest who enjoyed early mornings. He prepared to quell his disappointment at the disturbance, and was surprised when that wasn't one of the emotions filling him.

She wore her spectacles again, as she had at dinner the previous evening. In truth, he liked them—or was it just that he liked looking at her in general?

"Good morning." He rose and bowed briefly.

"And to you," she replied with a curtsy. She paused a moment longer then seemed to make up her mind and entered, despite his presence, moving quickly to the sideboard.

He sat and returned his attention to his meal, hoping to make it clear that conversation was unnecessary.

She placed a far too modest portion of food onto her plate, in his opinion, then sat two places down from him.

Clever of her, he decided, as the footman poured her tea. Close enough to converse if needed, and far enough away to allow him his privacy. Truly, she seemed to go out of her way not to be a bother in any respect. Perhaps that could be blamed for his sudden urge to be social.

"Did you sleep well?"

"I did. Travel was more tiring than I expected. Did you?"

"Well enough." He preferred to tell the truth

when possible. Sleep was something that eluded him most nights, until the cumulative lack of it hit him like a hammer.

She studied him briefly. "Did you travel a great distance to be here?"

"No." His lips clamped shut. They'd covered the basics of how they knew Adair and Grace during the intimate supper last night. But answering this question caused him to shift with embarrassment in his seat.

He'd rather not explain that his home was merely a short ride across the fields, though a longer distance if one followed the road. That he couldn't bear to remain there, alone, during the holidays. That explanation would only elicit the pity he so detested.

When he didn't add anything, she gave that single nod again. How she managed to put so much into that brief movement was beyond him. It was fascinating, really. That nod was graceful, intelligent, and respectful. It implied that she accepted his answer, or lack thereof, but would welcome additional details if he were so inclined.

What would it take to have her nod more? With enthusiasm? To put something other than polite interest in her expression? He cleared his throat, hoping it would clear his wayward thoughts as well. What on earth was wrong with him?

She remained silent, eating with efficiency, as though she did so to fuel her body and not for true enjoyment.

"Humph."

Her graceful movements with her fork and knife paused midair. "Excuse me?"

He glanced up in alarm, realizing the sound had not been silent, as he'd intended.

Her brow raised in question, her eyes, the color of warmed chocolate, resting on him.

Obviously, he'd spent too much time alone if he didn't realize when he was making such noises. His mind was blank, unable to think of an excuse.

"Just clearing my throat," he said at last.

"Of course." Her gaze returned to her plate.

He had the oddest urge to say something further so she'd look at him once again. He liked her eyes —the color, the shape, her lashes. With a frown, he stopped himself before he waxed poetic over them.

Miss Flitchard brought out the oddest responses in him. Before he could ponder the reasons, he heard voices and laughter drawing near.

Matthew, Grace's son, entered, followed by Adair and his bride, their attention focused on each other, hands linked. Their affection toward one another would take some getting used to. Most couples refrained from public displays. Perhaps it was their recent marriage or the intimacy of the house party or the holidays, but they showed no such restraint.

Cole couldn't help but glance at Miss Flitchard to see if she revealed any reaction to the pair. Her lips turned up and her eyes were even warmer as she watched their hosts. He'd have to say she was pleased by their behavior.

Cole rose, as did Miss Flitchard. "Good morning."

Adair grinned. "Please, no need for such formalities." He waved a hand for them to return to their seats. "I trust you both slept well?"

The conversation continued as they lingered over the simple meal.

"Cole, have you met Captain Hawke, Adair's brother?" Grace asked.

"I haven't yet had the pleasure."

"They'll arrive soon," Adair added. "You'll like Nathaniel and his wife."

"Uncle Nathaniel is grand," Matthew offered, clearly excited about the guests. "And Aunt Lettie is clever."

"Katherine hasn't met them yet either, though she's heard me speak of them many times," Grace said.

"I look forward to it," Katherine added. "Viscount Frost and his new bride are coming as well?"

The idea of being amidst several couples made Cole uncomfortable. A glance at Miss Flitchard showed a hint of dismay on her features as well. He hoped she didn't expect him to play the role of suitor with her.

It only took a moment for him to realize she expected no such thing, judging by the coolness of her expression as their gazes caught. Perhaps she didn't want to be paired with him either. The idea had him frowning.

"Are you available?" Adair's question pulled Cole out of his thoughts.

Cole glanced around the table as he felt the weight of their stares. Obviously, he'd missed much of the conversation. "Of course," he responded, only to realize he didn't know what he was answering to.

Grace rewarded him with a beaming smile. "Thank you so much. I just didn't realize the amount of greenery we'd need to decorate."

Adair's eyes narrowed while he watched Cole, as if he realized Cole had no idea what they were speaking about. "So kind of you and Miss Flitchard to gather it. I am certain you know the best place to collect holly and mistletoe."

"Mistletoe?" Gather greenery? With Miss Flitchard? Cole could only nod under the weight of everyone's stares, resigned to the outing.

He preferred holly. Mistletoe suggested kissing. His wayward thoughts had him glancing at Miss Flitchard again.

"We'll need it to make the kissing boughs." Grace shared a look with her husband that made Cole feel like an old prig for not wanting to collect it.

"Of course." Cole glanced at Miss Flitchard. "When would you like to go?"

She looked at Grace as though seeking her permission before she answered. At the countess's nod, she said, "I need only get my cloak and I'll be ready."

Cole hoped Adair wasn't sending him on some fool's errand merely for the purpose of throwing him together with the only other single guest.

Yet much to his surprise, he couldn't deny how much he looked forward to spending time with her. The appreciation she'd shown last night for the countryside made anticipation fill him at what she might find to admire today.

Adair arched a brow in response, acting the innocent.

With a sigh, Cole sipped the last of his coffee and decided he needed to have a conversation with Adair to clarify that neither he nor his wife should make any attempt at matchmaking during the house party.

His focus was to put one foot in front of the other, living each day as it came. The future was something he avoided thinking about at all costs.

Katherine found herself sitting beside Lord Barclay, or rather Cole, as he'd insisted she call him, this time in a brake drawn by two horses with room to carry the greenery in the back. The crisp air held a hint of frost this morning but no suggestion of snow.

She raised the hood of her cloak, pleased to find warmed bricks at their feet. Grace had handed her a muff as she'd seen them off. Katherine appreciated the small comforts, things to which she was no longer accustomed.

She was still confused as to why she and Cole had been enlisted to gather greenery. As many servants as there were in Crawford House, it was hard to imagine they were all too busy with other duties to be enlisted for this chore.

But Grace appeared so nervous that the party wouldn't go as planned, or the house wouldn't look festive enough, that Katherine hadn't been able to refuse her.

"Is it very far?" she asked as Cole flicked the reins.

"No."

The abruptness of his answer made her realize that he didn't care to go on this outing. Well, that made two of them. She wasn't much of a person for the outdoors, though that term referred to something completely different in London than it did here.

She determined to hold her silence until spoken to. She adjusted her spectacles, wishing she hadn't worn them. The things were a nuisance but had been part of her disguise as a seamstress. Grace expected Miss Flitchard to wear them, and no matter how many times Katherine had thought it over, she had yet to find a way to explain that she was actually Mrs. Flemming, a widow of three years. She disliked deceiving Grace in any way, but did it really matter what her friend believed for the short time she'd be here? Besides, the fewer people who knew her real name, the better.

Her mood shifted, lifting, as the brisk, clean air filled her lungs, clearing the cobwebs of worry from her mind and invigorating her. Unfortunately, there wasn't any snow to complete the picture, but the frost on the grass and foliage combined with the sun emerging from the clouds created a picturesque scene. Added to that was the jingle from the horses' harnesses, echoing in the quiet of the countryside.

How could anyone remain in a poor frame of mind when surrounded by all this?

"It's quite beautiful." She said it to herself but wished she would've only thought it, for Cole's gaze swung toward her.

After studying her for a long moment, causing her already warm cheeks to heat further, he looked back out across the rolling fields.

Perhaps this sort of view was something he was used to. It seemed a shame that anyone would take this for granted.

The thought made her look at the handsome man sitting so close to her from beneath her lashes. There had been a few times at breakfast when he'd appeared fully engaged in what was happening around him, but equally as many when he'd been immersed in his thoughts. Based on the shutter that came down over his features, she had to assume they weren't good thoughts. Like now. Though tempted to draw him into conversation, she decided against doing so. Instead of worrying over him, she should focus on planning for what happened next in her life.

Six months at a time. That was what she had, assuming she was clever with her new identity and position. Then he'd find her, and she'd have to do it all over again.

The man beside her cleared his throat, drawing her back to the present. "My property starts just there." He raised a gloved hand to point to a line of trees on the horizon.

"You live nearby?"

"Do you see the thatched cottage at the edge of the trees?" He pointed to the spot.

"Oh, it's charming. Like something out of a storybook." The cottage, with its whitewashed walls and thatched roof, looked like it had been transported from medieval times.

"It's empty. Has been for well over a year now. That's where my land starts. The best place to gather holly and the like is on the northern border between Adair's land and mine."

The way he said "mine" had her studying him closer. What would it be like to think of the land as far as you could see as yours? The idea was inconceivable to her. Since her husband's death, all she owned could be easily packed into her two bags.

"It *is* beautiful," he said as his gaze swept from the view to her, the intensity of his hazel eyes causing a flutter deep inside her. "Sometimes I forget."

She nodded. "I suppose when you see something every day, that's to be expected."

"It's good to be reminded of its beauty. I take it for granted." A puff of steam emerged as his warm breath hit the cool air.

She waited, hoping he'd say more. She liked listening to his deep, quiet voice. He placed emphasis on certain vowels that must be common in those who lived in this area but, to her city ears, sounded almost lyrical.

The silence between them was no longer awkward, as though now that they'd found common ground, even in just this one small area, they were comfortable together.

However, the continued silence didn't stop her from wondering about him. Pain lingered in the back of his eyes, of that she had no doubt, for she saw it in her mirror every day. She couldn't help but wonder what had caused his.

Before long, they approached a copse of trees. She'd never gathered greenery before and had no idea how to go about it. Once he halted the horses and secured them, he came to her side and offered his hand.

"I must confess that I haven't done this before." She reached the ground, her eyes lifting to meet his. He was taller than she remembered, his broad shoulders appearing even broader in his thick wool coat. She reprimanded herself, determined to stop thinking about this man in such an intimate manner. "I'm not certain how to help."

"I have no doubt you'll be a quick learner." He retrieved a small saw from under the seat and gestured toward the trees. "Shall we?"

"Did you know the tradition of decorating with holly and other greens dates back to Roman times?"

"And here you said you wouldn't be of any help."

The teasing light in his sparkling eyes made her catch her breath. It had been a long time since a man had looked at her thusly.

"Yes, well, since I don't know where to find it, nor can I promise to recognize it if I see it, I must argue."

He stopped to face her. "You don't decorate your home with greenery during the holidays?"

Before she could think of a lie, she shook her head. "Not since I was a young girl." Her husband hadn't cared for the holidays, insisting it was a waste of time, and money was better spent on investments than trivial decorations or gifts.

A small pucker briefly appeared between his brows, but much to her relief, he didn't comment. "Look for red berries. That will lead us to where we need to go." He glanced around the trees. "My mother loved holly."

She would've missed the shadow of pain that flashed over his features if she hadn't been watching him so closely. The question on the tip of her tongue died a quick death. She had no desire to bring that shadow back by asking a question better left alone.

Chapter Four

Cole felt Miss Flitchard's presence with every bone in his body as he led the way down a narrow path into a copse of bare-branched oaks and holly bushes.

Too late, he realized he should've brought a servant with them. Or Matthew. He'd forgotten how intimate this part of the woods was, hidden from sight. No matter. They'd cut the holly, load the brake, and return to Crawford House in short order.

He stopped to look up, searching for the best limbs. "You have gloves?"

"Yes." She turned around in a slow circle, her excited gaze sweeping the area in awe. "This is amazing. But why are the ones with the most berries so high?"

Cole couldn't help but smile, for he'd been thinking the same thing.

"How do you propose we gather it?" Her expression held as much doubt as her tone.

It had been years since Cole had performed this task. He studied the options as memories of doing this with his sister came to mind. A deep ache filled him. He missed her so much. It was still inconceivable that he would never see her or his mother and father again.

Over the past two years, since their unexpected deaths from influenza, he'd brutally shoved aside any memories that came to mind. The pain was too overwhelming.

But somehow today was different. Whether it was Miss Flitchard's presence, her smile, or obvious delight at the task before them, he couldn't say.

"My sister, Megan, and I used to come to this spot every year to gather holly." He closed his eyes for a moment as a familiar wave of loss slid through him. But for once, it left behind the warmth of a memory.

When he opened his eyes, he was careful to keep his gaze well away from Miss Flitchard. He didn't want to answer any questions. He knew she had them, for he felt the weight of her stare. She was far too observant in his opinion.

Those who knew him had learned that speaking of his past was not permitted. Allowing a memory to sneak past his defenses didn't change that.

"I'm going to climb this oak." Appreciating her silence, he pointed to the one that looked like it would both support him and provide the necessary reach. "I should be able to cut the holly and hand it down to you. Then I'll move over to another and re-peat the process."

"Excellent." She gave that single nod again. Damn if it didn't stir something deep within him.

With determination, he shoved aside his inter-est and climbed the tree. From his perch, he looked down at her. "Will you hand me the saw?"

Miss Flitchard did as he requested then waited with arms ready to catch the holly.

Hearing his mother's whispers in his mind, he was careful not to cut too much from any one place. She'd always insisted they take care not to damage the holly tree so it would grow again the next year. The bright, glossy bunches of deep green with their cheerful red berries were festive, though the difficulty in collecting them made the job a chore.

"Shall I take these to the brake and return for more?" Miss Flitchard called up to him.

He glanced down to see the top of her head barely visible above the pile in her arms. Perhaps he'd overdone it. He should've sent her to the brake several branches ago. "Only if you feel able."

She gave a muffled reply and tottered away with her load.

He continued cutting and moving, watching for his assistant's return. When at last she did, he didn't question the relief that filled him.

"My, you've been busy." She started gathering the bunches. "Ouch!"

"Take care," he called down. "It helps if you don't clutch them too tightly."

"Funny how something so beautiful can be so prickly. It reminds me of many of the ladies in London."

He chuckled at her remark, wondering if her experience as a seamstress made her say such a thing. When silence was the only thing that greeted his ears, he glanced down to see the clearing empty once again. She must've taken another load to the brake.

As he climbed down the oak to find another place to cut holly, she returned.

"I know this is holly, but what does mistletoe look like?" she asked, those lovely brown eyes looking at him from behind her lenses. The scent of lilacs drifted toward him, a heady fragrance when mixed with the greenery and fresh, clean air.

His gaze held hers, his mind blank. It had been a long time since he'd stood this close to an attractive woman. The curve of her rosy cheeks, the strong line of her jaw, the pink tip of her nose—all drew his notice. The tight bun of her hair had loosened, softening the lines of her face.

She'd unfastened the top of her cloak after her trips to the brake. Once again, she wore a brown dress, but what should've been unremarkable pulled his attention to the smoothness of her creamy skin. Her dark brows arched over those fascinating eyes.

Which blinked up at him as the silence drew long.

At last his mind caught up with the conversation. "Mistletoe?" Since words seemed beyond him, he searched for it to show her. "There. Up high. Do you see it?"

Her gaze followed his finger, but she shook her head. "I'm not certain what I'm looking for."

Her upturned face revealed the graceful line of

her neck. The opening of her cloak exposed the slight dip where her collarbones met, which pulsed slightly. The idea of pressing his lips to that spot prevented any other thoughts from forming.

But when her gaze swung to him again, he drew a quick breath to free his senses from her spell.

He positioned himself behind her, one hand on her shoulder as he moved her forward, pointing to the mistletoe above them. "The one with the white berries."

She shifted closer to align her sight with his finger. "I see it."

"It's parasitic, so it grows on other plants rather than on its own."

She turned her head to look at him, her eyes seeing deep inside him, her lips curving into a small smile. The small scar at the corner of her eye made his stomach flip. "It doesn't want to be lonely either."

Either? Did that mean she was lonely? The emptiness deep inside him shifted, coming to life as though to remind him that he was too, no matter how hard he tried to deny it.

Mouth suddenly dry, he could only stare at her, his body aching as longing coursed through him.

Katherine's breath caught. What had possessed her to say such a thing? Besides, she wasn't lonely. She was surrounded by people every day, helping customers at the modiste's. Granted, none of them were her friends, or acknowledged her existence most of the time.

Except Grace. She'd seen past her quiet demeanor and effort to blend in, right to her heart.

The look in Cole's eyes made her wonder if he did the same. She told herself to step away and gain some distance from his intoxicating presence. She couldn't think of the last time she'd stood so close to a handsome man, let alone spoken with one.

Her wayward body ignored her and turned to face him fully, close enough to see the green and gold flecks in the depths of his hazel eyes. Long lashes guarded those eyes, often sweeping down to hide his thoughts. But not now.

In this moment, he looked at her without the shutters. Shadows still lurked in their depths, but perhaps not as dark as before.

A shaving from a branch he'd cut rested on his cheek. With slow, stilted movements, she reached up to wipe it away. His gaze fell to her lips, hiding his thoughts once again. But the idea of him staring at her mouth had her drawing a quick breath.

Yes.

Kiss me.

The thought surprised her. This man was a stranger, albeit a handsome one. Yet she couldn't get the idea out of her mind.

It had been a long time since anyone had touched her, let alone with desire. Was it so wrong to want to be desired?

"Miss Flitchard." His whispered words made her close her eyes with regret.

She couldn't bear for him to use her false name. In this moment, she didn't want lies to stand between them.

"Katherine," he amended, his voice hoarse. Her given name in his deep tone sent shivers of longing flowing through her.

"Yes." She hoped he understood her meaning, that she was giving him permission.

He eased even closer, until the steam of their breath in the cool air mingled. Then he pressed his mouth to hers. His lips were surprisingly warm. Firm. Heavenly.

He lingered there a moment, nibbling slightly as though to better taste her. Then his tongue swept inside, making her legs weak. The heady feelings flooding her body were marvelous. She'd forgotten what desire could feel like. While her husband had been older than her, her affection for him had made their marriage bed pleasurable.

But this was something different. Something... more. So much more.

She jerked back at that realization. She was not looking for more. Nor could she.

"My first kiss beneath mistletoe," she said. "Thank you." She quickly bent to pick up the holly before the magic of the mistletoe combined with Cole caused more problems.

Chapter Five

"To the left." Grace's eyes narrowed as she studied the garland Katherine held above the fireplace mantel. "A bit higher. Perfect."

Katherine sighed with relief. Her arms ached from repeating this same routine in every room of the house. The immense pile of greenery she and Cole had brought back yesterday was nearly gone.

Grace was determined to make this Christmas perfect. That meant completing the decorating, as the other guests were to arrive tomorrow.

"I don't know what I'd do without you." Grace squeezed Katherine's arm. "Thank you so much for all your help."

"It's my pleasure." Katherine smiled. "I haven't done anything like this before. It is tremendous work, but great fun."

Upon returning to the house after that heated kiss with Cole, Katherine had spent a restless night trying to determine if she should leave. The fairy-tale feeling created by the amazing estate with a countess and an earl, far from the city, topped off by kissing a handsome baron, was dangerous, luring her into wishing for things that couldn't be. Since her arrival, her world had been askew. Nothing was as she'd expected.

But in the early morning hours, she'd decided to embrace it. Why not enjoy this one magical holiday? It would be a memory to tuck away and cherish in the years to come. For once, she was surrounded by people she truly liked. Instead of waiting on customers and stitching late into the night, she was decorating this beautiful home with a dear friend.

And she loved it.

Reality had suspended. Rather than worrying about what the next day would bring, she was going to spread cheer as best she could, right alongside Grace.

She'd decided to make Cole her primary objective. He'd been so uncomfortable after their kiss, as though he feared she'd demand marriage or request that Adair confront him. Silly man. It was only a kiss.

But, oh, what a kiss.

Her stomach filled with butterflies at the memory.

Not that she intended to repeat it. The idea held far too much risk.

That didn't mean she wouldn't do all she could to push away those shadows in his eyes, even temporarily.

"Now for this kissing bough." Grace slowly walked around the drawing room. "Where would be the best place for it?"

Katherine considered the options. "Do you want it in a place that will likely cause trouble, or tucked away for more intimate use?"

"Trouble?" Grace laughed. "That's one way to think of it. Just be sure you don't refuse a kiss if you find yourself underneath it."

Katherine smiled as she trailed a finger along the holly and ivy wound with mistletoe that rested on the table. "Cole said mistletoe is a parasite."

"That's a terribly unromantic thing to say."

"I don't know. I think it rather sweet that the plant prefers not to grow alone. It seeks companionship."

Grace caught her breath. "That is one of the many reasons I adore you. You look at things differently than anyone else."

Katherine waved a hand. "Please. I'm the most ordinary person you'll ever meet." She swallowed hard, all too aware the Katherine that Grace knew was made of lies. She dearly wanted to tell her the truth about everything.

The days she spent here had only deepened her affection for Grace. She would miss her when she left, for she doubted she'd have the chance to see her again. Miss Flitchard would disappear. Katherine would invent a new identity, learn a new occupation, and they would never cross paths again.

"I'll bet Cole didn't mention that fact to be romantic."

"No." In fact, he'd gone out of his way to avoid her since their return, making her goal of spreading Christmas cheer difficult. Romance was the last thing on that man's mind.

"If you do share a kiss, you must remove a berry," Grace warned. "Once all the berries are gone, no more kisses can be taken, so don't wait too long to enjoy yours."

Unthinking, Katherine reached out to pluck a white berry from the bough. While she wouldn't call herself superstitious, she'd already shared a kiss under the mistletoe in the woods.

Grace's gasp made Katherine realize what she'd revealed.

"I knew it." Grace touched Katherine's shoulder, eyes wide. "I thought I sensed something upon your return after gathering greenery with Cole."

Katherine's cheeks heated at the accusation, but she said nothing. How she hated the lies she had to tell each and every day. She couldn't bring herself to deny the kiss and tell another. Not to Grace.

"He acted uncomfortable upon your return." Grace clapped her hands. "That is delightful. I can't think of two people more deserving of a little light in their lives than both of you."

Katherine had no doubt Cole deserved happiness, but she wasn't so certain about herself. She didn't think she could forgive herself for her past mistakes. Guilt and regret were her companions, and she had no idea how to shed them. Perhaps she wasn't meant to. Perhaps those two emotions were her punishment.

"Please don't push us together." Katherine

couldn't help but caution her friend, wanting to plead with her. But wouldn't that make the kiss seem more important than it had been? "It was just one kiss."

She rolled the berry between her fingers, trying to push aside the longing that washed through her.

And that was all it would be.

The regret that knowledge brought squeezed her heart.

Cole retrieved another box of decorations from the attic, glancing about to make sure it was the last one. The house had more decorations than any he'd ever seen. Boxes and boxes had been hauled downstairs and emptied under Grace's direction, with Katherine right beside her.

"Is that the last of it?" Adair asked as he appeared in the doorway.

"I believe so."

"I have no idea where the ladies are putting all these."

"It's a large house, and your bride seems determined to decorate each and every room."

Adair laughed. "She's quite excited."

"You're a lucky man." Adair and Grace together were delightful. Their joy in each other, their appreciation for what they had, was wonderful.

"I am *so* lucky." Adair stared across the attic, obviously seeing something Cole couldn't. "I never thought a life like this was possible."

Cole wondered what he meant by that, but hesitated to ask. It was none of his business. He liked Adair well enough, but he wasn't here to bond with the man. Only to escape his demons and perhaps buy a mare.

Adair looked back at him. "I hope all these preparations aren't making you feel worse. I haven't told Grace of your loss, but perhaps I should so she doesn't drag you into every possible holiday activity."

Cole wasn't certain which was worse.

Each Christmas tradition Grace seemed intent on arranging brought memories of doing so with his family. The heavy weight of pain in his chest made it difficult to move. To breathe. To think. To live.

What was that terrible saying? *Time heals all wounds*? It was rubbish, as far as Cole was concerned.

The choice Adair offered was none at all.

One thing he knew for certain was that he didn't want Katherine to know. He didn't want the look in those melted chocolate eyes to change to pity. He much preferred the interest that warred with caution reflected in their depths.

Thank heaven for the caution. Katherine had a reserve about her that suggested she had a few secrets of her own. Maybe his interest in her was more about curiosity.

Ha. He nearly scoffed out loud at the thought. He was self-aware enough to admit that he was attracted to her on every level possible. Except for the part where that meant opening himself to feelings he'd locked tight in a box and shoved in the attic of his mind.

Suddenly aware of Adair's steady regard, Cole shook his head, bringing himself back to the box in his arms and the dusty attic. And Adair's question.

"It makes no difference. I'll leave that to your judgment. I'll be fine." Wasn't he always? Whether he willed it or not, he remained in good health, rising each day, placing one foot in front of the other.

Alone.

This fortnight was a brief respite from his own company. No doubt once it was over, he'd be eager to return to the solitude of his home.

"Very well." Adair nodded, his grey eyes watchful. "Do let me know if you change your mind."

That evening, Katherine entered the drawing room, where it had become a habit for them to gather for conversation and a drink prior to supper. This would be the last one with only the four of them.

Her stomach gave a little jolt as she spotted Cole standing near the fireplace, a crystal glass filled with amber liquid cupped in his hand. He was turned partially away from her, his expression somber as he stared into the dancing flames. The shadows made his broad shoulders appear massive, his hips narrow. He was obviously an active man who spent much of his time outdoors. Much different from the pasty, overweight lords and merchants she often encountered in London.

His dark hair was smoothed to the side, the back of it clipped short. While a thin layer of civility covered him, there was no denying the virile man hidden by his black suit.

The notion gave her a little shiver. What would it be like to see that strength and power unleashed?

His gaze swung to her as though sensing her presence. "Good evening," he said, straightening to face her.

"How was your day?" She moved forward, hands folded before her.

"Filled with more fetching and carrying." He said the words with a small smile, as though he hadn't minded his tasks overmuch. Without asking, he moved to the sideboard to pour her a small glass of sherry. "And yours?"

"Much the same." She took the glass, her fingers brushing his. What might it feel like to hold his strong hand in hers? She had noted the calluses on his palms, the small scuffs and scars that showed how active he truly was. He might be a nobleman, but he wasn't an idle one.

Her breath caught as he trailed a finger along her cheek to tuck a strand of hair behind her ear. That simple touch sent desire flooding through her.

"Surely Grace can't find another place to decorate." Cole glanced at the greenery flowing out of a square crystal vase on the sideboard as he stepped back.

Katherine chuckled, trying to regain her balance. "I wouldn't be so sure. Each time I think everything looks perfect, she finds something else."

She hoped he didn't take this chance to try to learn more about her. Despite their kiss, she was still intimidated that he was a lord. What could they possibly have in common? Thus far, she'd told him as little about herself as possible without being rude.

"Do you spend all your time in Northamptonshire?" Better to shift the conversation before he asked any questions.

He was silent for a long moment. "I have for the past two years." He took a sip of his drink, the shadows in his eyes back in full force. "I traveled for a time after university."

"Your grand tour?" At his nod, she added, "That must've been an amazing experience."

"Parts of it were. What of you? Have you ventured far?"

Her cheeks heated as she glanced down at her drink. "You'll think me quite unsophisticated, but this is the farthest I've traveled from London."

"Did the opportunity not present itself, or do you prefer to stay close to home?" He watched her as though quite curious.

"The opportunity never arose." The truth was that her family hadn't had the resources to do so. Her father had been moderately successful in the banking business. That provided them with a comfortable home and lifestyle but not enough to travel.

Her husband had been quite wealthy but insisted travel didn't agree with him.

"You say that as though any possibility has come and gone."

She should've realized how astute he was and guarded her words more carefully. How she hated the lies. "My life has changed much in the past few years, so I'm doubtful of the chance."

He waited, remaining silent and watchful, as though allowing her to expand on her comment if she wished. But he didn't ask any further questions.

"I hope we haven't kept you waiting." Adair glanced at Grace as they walked into the room. "She was making me rearrange the garland in our bedroom."

Grace laughed. "I just want everything perfect." She reached up to touch his cheek. "Especially for you."

The love in their eyes as they looked at each other sent a sharp pang through Katherine. She drew a deep breath, hoping to release its grasp around her heart.

A small sound had her turning to look at Cole. For a brief moment, she had the oddest notion he felt the same.

Was that the reason for the sadness in his eyes? Loneliness? Then perhaps they had more in common than she thought. If only she could determine

a way to ease that during their brief time here together.

Chapter Six

The next evening, after the guests settled in, they enjoyed a meal of roast beef with potatoes and gravy and baked apples for dessert, followed by games in the drawing room.

Cole had never felt so uncomfortable in his life. Captain Hawke and his bride were friendly, as were Viscount Frost and his new wife. He enjoyed their company.

But playing charades and "pass the slipper" held far too many memories of Christmas past with his family.

He rose from the group with the excuse of refilling his wassail cup and slipped out the garden door to clear his head. Unfortunately, the memories came with him. His sister had adored charades, and he remembered laughing with her until his cheeks hurt. He rubbed his chest at the ache the memory brought.

"Is all well?" Katherine asked as she joined him, running her hands over her bare arms to chase away the cold. Obviously, she'd learned of his past if she'd followed him out here.

"Just needed some fresh air." Cole turned to face

her, bracing himself for the pity.

"I'm pleased you did, for it gave me an excuse to do the same." She smiled at him then looked up at the night sky.

Her profile, including the long line of her neck, drew his gaze. "Need an escape?"

"They are all just so...happy." She turned to look at him as though hoping he understood.

"It is nice to see but hard to watch."

"Exactly," she agreed.

He removed his suit coat and placed it over her shoulders, noticing how her gaze fell to his mouth.

"Thank you. You didn't have to do that."

"My pleasure." It gave him an excuse to draw nearer. He dearly wanted another kiss. "Did you play those games as a child?"

"Yes. They're still fun, aren't they?"

He held his silence.

"No?"

"They remind me of better times." He hoped she'd let it go at that.

She reached up to place her gloved hand on his chest. "Yes."

That single word expressed so much. Understanding. Agreement. Empathy. His skin heated where she touched him. He gave into his desire and kissed her, long and deep. The vividness of his memories faded, allowing his mind to fill with the woman in his arms.

Though his relief might be only temporary, he appreciated it all the same. Yet he worried Katherine would have false hope for the future, and that was something he couldn't offer.

"Katherine—"

"Shh." She reached up to place a finger on his lips and gently smiled. "No regrets. No excuses. It's Christmas, and that was just a kiss."

Just a kiss? If that were true, why did he feel as if he never wanted to let her go?

The next day, Katherine admired the bow-front windows of the jewelry shop, full of pretty gift ideas. The guests had wanted to explore the village all decked in its Christmas finery.

It had been a long time since she'd had the chance to window-shop, other than glancing at the displays of the stores near the modiste's.

Clouds hung heavy in the sky this afternoon. An extra dampness that hadn't been there yesterday lingered in the air. Might that mean the possibility of snow?

She smiled at the thought, which made her as giddy as a schoolgirl. It was impossible to be in a foul mood in this village. The scents, sounds, and sights of the holiday were everywhere—from the greenery hanging above shop doors, to the cinnamon scent that wafted through the air, to the hums of Christmas carols from other shoppers.

While she was grateful for a chance to explore the village, the little money she had needed to be saved for her new life. She'd already made a keep-sake box for Grace and found a toy train whistle for Matthew. Those would have to be the extent of her gift giving this year.

A bank account in her name had significant funds, but accessing it alerted her husband's brother. She could only surmise he'd convinced someone at the bank that she was a gold digger who'd murdered her husband and gotten away with it. The thought made her ill.

She preferred to earn her own way, though that was no easy feat when she was chased from position to position every few months.

The other ladies in the party were just ahead of her, Grace included. Their laughter drew Katherine's eye. Their high spirits lifted her yet made her all the more aware of her solitary existence.

"Katherine? Are you coming?" Grace called.

As she moved forward, Katherine sensed the weight of someone's gaze across the street. She glanced over to see a man standing in the doorway of a shop. Something about the way he stared had Katherine turning away even as her heart leapt.

Markus?

Could it be? Surely not.

Her hands shook as she followed Grace and the other ladies inside. She positioned herself far enough from the window that no one could see her but she had a view of the street.

Her pulse skittered as she searched the area. How could he have found her so quickly? Where could she go? What could she do?

"Is something amiss?" Grace's whispered question had Katherine turning to face her.

Katherine drew a breath to calm herself. Giving into her fear wouldn't get her anywhere. Above all, she didn't want her murky past to ruin Grace's Christmas. Not after all the hard work she'd put into the preparations.

"I thought I saw someone I knew, but it was nothing."

"Are you certain? You've gone pale." Grace's dark eyes were full of concern.

In many ways, it only made Katherine feel worse. How could she call Grace a friend when Grace didn't even know her real name? She'd known Grace had questions from that first day Katherine and the modiste had visited her home on Grosvenor Square. Grace had never pressed her for the truth. She'd only reached out in friendship.

Katherine had responded with lies.

But what choice did she have? She couldn't bear the idea of Grace learning how Katherine had been suspected of aiding in her husband's death. A wealthy, older husband. Markus, Walter's brother, had deemed her a gold digger from the moment he'd met her. He'd disapproved of the marriage and done all in his power to convince his brother that Katherine was an unsuitable bride and a thief.

Walter had dismissed his allegations and married Katherine anyway. They'd spent several pleasant years together until he'd fallen ill. Then everything had gone wrong.

Katherine didn't want to remember that dark time.

Nor could she bear for Grace to look at her with suspicion in her eyes, as so many others had.

She'd need to leave soon. But where? If only she'd planned her next identity and position rather than celebrating the holiday. Such frivolous behavior was not for her. What had she been thinking?

If that was Markus and he'd caught sight of her, she needed to make a quick escape. Did she dare return to Crawford House?

"I am not feeling my best." Katherine swallowed hard as she told yet another lie. "I think I'll go back to the house and rest."

"Oh, no. Take one of the carriages and send it back. I don't think the other ladies are done shopping yet."

"Thank you."

When Grace gave her a warm hug, a lump formed in Katherine's throat. She'd miss Grace more than she had anyone in a long time when she had to leave.

"Feel better. We'll see you soon."

Katherine nodded. With luck, she'd be able to escape Markus's notice and return to Crawford House. She searched out the window but saw no sign of him. Gathering her courage, she stepped onto the walkway and drew up the hood of her cloak, hoping to make herself less recognizable.

The carriage waited at the end of the street. A man stepped onto the walkway between her and the carriage.

Markus.

Katherine spun around to walk in the opposite direction, heart racing.

Dear heavens. There was no doubt it was him. Whatever could she do now?

Cole sighed as he glanced up and down the main street of the village. He'd nearly remained behind but remembered he had yet to select a gift for his hosts. A splendid wooden toy train was already tucked away for Matthew. And he'd found a cameo pin for Katherine. Should he try to pick several little trinkets for the other guests as well?

The small town was bustling today. Christmas was only three days away. Smoke billowed out of the baker's chimney, bringing with it the scent of gingerbread and an idea. Perhaps some sort of treat might be appropriate to give each couple.

As he headed in that direction, he realized how many strangers were on the walkways. The holidays always brought relatives to town, but he knew many of them. A sign of the prosperity of the area, he supposed, that more people were making their homes here, which meant more strangers.

He preferred it the way it had been.

"Good day to you, Lord Barclay." The baker's wife's rounded face was lit with a smile and the heat of the oven.

"Business is brisk today, eh?"

She leaned forward as she wiped her hands on her apron. "It's both a blessing and a curse."

He made his selections, and she wrapped each in brown paper.

"Many strangers are roaming the village," he remarked as she worked.

"A few of them are downright rude, asking all sorts of questions about the earl and his new wife." She shook her head in disgust even as her fingers flew, tying each of his packages with string.

"Oh?" Cole didn't care for the sound of that. "Was it someone in particular?"

"A man, a few years older than you, I'd say. By the way he's dressed and his accent, he must be from London. Looked down his nose at our little village."

"What sort of information was he asking?"

"He wanted to know about the earl's guests."

Cole reached for the wrapped bundles, dismissing the woman's worries. "Probably just curious."

"He also wanted to know if there was a young woman amongst the guests. One that would've recently arrived from London alone. Said she had some skill as a seamstress."

Cole paused, his senses on high alert. That described Katherine. Could this man be searching for her for some reason?

Mrs. Barnaby shook her head. "I'd say he doesn't feel an ounce of affection for the woman. He seemed almost angry, as if he resented having to come all this way to find her."

"What did you tell him?"

"That I didn't know who the earl had invited for the holidays, and even if I did, I wouldn't share that with a stranger." She gave a nod. "Hopefully that will have him thinking twice before he goes around to the other merchants asking such things."

"Well done, Mrs. Barnaby. Will you let me know if he returns? Send word to Crawford House, as I'm staying there over the holidays."

Cole took his leave, glancing up and down the walkway with the faint hope of finding Katherine. Surely she'd want to know someone was searching for her.

He caught sight of Grace leaving the jewelry store and hurried toward her.

"Katherine returned to the house. She said she wasn't feeling well and was going to rest."

The news should've relaxed Cole, but the nagging worry continued. As he waited for the other guests, he walked slowly up and down the street but didn't find a man fitting Mrs. Barnaby's description.

That didn't reassure him either. He couldn't release his unease.

A bell chimed from the door of a shop behind him, and he turned to see a man step out.

The man's somber expression seemed out of place in the festive atmosphere of the village. And his dark hair and suit matched Mrs. Barnaby's description.

"Excuse me," Cole said, determined to find out what the man was about. This was his village, at least he considered it so, and he had no intention of allowing a stranger to upset anyone in it. "Did I hear you were searching for someone?"

The man's cool blue eyes held Cole's for a long moment before he answered. "Yes, perhaps you can assist me." He pulled a pocket watch out of his vest and clicked it open. "Have you seen this woman?"

A picture of Katherine with an older man was tucked inside. It was a younger version of her, but there was no mistaking the arch of her brow or the curve of her cheek. "Who is she?"

The man clenched his jaw with impatience. "A relative. Have you seen her?"

Cole studied the picture again, noting the resemblance between the man in the photograph and this man. Brothers, perhaps? "I haven't seen her. It's a small village. If she'd been here, I'd know."

"Humph." The man snapped the watch closed. "Thank you."

Cole wanted to tell him to leave, to search elsewhere, and leave Katherine alone. He didn't know why he was looking for her, but he didn't care for the man's attitude.

Cole knew Katherine had secrets. He'd noticed several things that didn't make sense. While she answered to "Katherine" readily enough, she rarely answered the first time to "Miss Flitchard." And he wondered if her spectacles were an attempt to disguise her appearance, as she often forgot them.

But none of that mattered. He liked her. If he hadn't been so busy trying to keep his distance, perhaps he'd have discovered more about her.

"Happy Christmas," Cole called as the man turned and strode away.

He didn't answer.

Cole strode toward the waiting carriage, acting on instinct. "Did Miss Flitchard ask to be driven back to the house?"

"No," the waiting footman said. "We haven't seen her, my lord."

Snowflakes drifted down, large and fluffy, the clouds finally releasing their heavy burden. Katherine was out in this deteriorating weather that appeared to be settling in for the remainder of the day.

He had to find her quickly, but where to begin the search?

Chapter Seven

Katherine was chilled to the bone. She shivered with each step, keeping her pace brisk with the hope of quickly reaching her destination as well as staying warm. But it wasn't working.

How ironic that the snow she'd wished for had arrived at the worst possible time. She wasn't certain of the whereabouts of the quaint little cottage she'd first seen on her outing with Cole. It was the only place she could think of to hide, as it was off the road and would provide shelter.

When Markus had blocked her path to the carriage, she'd panicked, terrified he'd follow her to Grace's. She couldn't allow the unpleasantness of her past to sully their first Christmas. But she hadn't planned on the snow. Or the cold.

He hadn't followed her out of the village, so she assumed he hadn't seen her. Unwilling to risk being caught, she'd decided the cottage was her best option. She clutched her cloak tighter, yet still the cold flakes found their way inside. Cole had said it didn't snow often. Surely that meant it would soon stop.

The field was already coated in white. Her boots

weren't meant for tramping through field or snow, let alone both. Her toes had gone numb, and her fingers nearly were as well.

With determination, she pushed back the panic to think. She turned to look toward the village. At this point, she was certain the closest shelter was the cottage. The practical thing to do was continue toward it.

The snow limited her vision when the wind picked up. She could only hope she was moving in the right direction. Some of the landmarks here looked familiar, such as that fallen tree. She hurried faster, hoping she was right.

Relief swept through her at the welcome sight of the cottage. Within a few short minutes, she reached for the latch, hoping it wasn't locked. For once, luck was on her side.

She closed the door behind her, pleased to be out of the blowing snow. Her eyes adjusted slowly to the dim interior. The pleasant fragrance of herbs filled the air, easing the musty smell of disuse.

Rubbing her arms, she walked through the two small rooms. A table and chairs and shelves were in one corner, making up the kitchen. Two oversized, tufted chairs sat before the empty fireplace. The other, smaller room contained a narrow bed, nightstand, and bureau.

The place might look cozy, but it was freezing. A woodbin stood empty beside the fireplace, but even if she had wood, building a fire would only signal to someone that she was here. The idea of being discovered by Markus sent waves of fear coursing through her.

She didn't need a fire. Though as she trembled yet again, she couldn't help but worry. A few hours in the cold would do her no harm, she assured herself. The snow would soon stop, darkness would fall, and she could walk to Crawford House. And pray that Markus had given up and left the area.

She peeked out a dusty window, only to see the snow still falling. Her breath frosted the glass pane, dimming her view.

With a sigh, she pulled the only blanket, coarse and dusty, off the bed. She sought a chair before the empty fire, shivering and tired. So tired. Tired of running and lying and keeping her distance from everyone she met.

Tears filled her eyes, and for once, she let them fall.

Cole turned his face from the blinding snow, praying he was doing the right thing. When he'd returned to Crawford House to find that Katherine had not come back, he'd been terrified. The storm's fierceness had taken them all by surprise. It rarely snowed this hard in Northamptonshire.

Cole, Adair, the other male guests, and many of the servants had ventured out to search for her between Crawford House and the village, but to no avail. Cole had told Adair he had an idea of where she might be, since they hadn't found any sign of her along the road.

Adair had offered to accompany him, but Cole opted to go alone. If he was wrong, they'd need to launch another search. Adair and the others could rest and warm themselves while he checked the cottage.

His horse didn't seem to appreciate the blinding snow any more than he did, but its steady pace despite the conditions was much appreciated. The cottage should be just ahead. The snow was disorienting, even for him, and he knew where he was going. The chance of Katherine finding it seemed slim.

Relief filled him when the small building came into view. But no smoke billowed out of the chimney.

Damn.

He paused, wondering where else he could search. Then he remembered how much of a city person Katherine was. Would she know where to find wood or kindling? To his recollection, the cottage wasn't stocked with much of anything. He needed to rectify that in case someone sought shelter there in the future.

With a press of his knees, he urged his steed toward the cottage, deciding to check inside, since he was this close.

He left his horse loosely tied in the small overhang attached to the building, where it would be sheltered from most of the weather. After a quick knock on the door, he pushed it open. "Hello?"

A glance about showed nothing disturbed since the last time he'd been there. Disappointment laced with a healthy dose of fear poured through him. If she wasn't here, he had no idea where she might be.

"C-C-Cole?" His stuttered name was barely audible above the roar of the wind.

"Katherine?" He hadn't seen her tucked in the chair in the dark shadows by the empty fireplace. "Are you well?"

"J-just c-cold."

He shut the door and hurried forward, alarmed at how pale she was now that his eyes had adjusted to the dim light. It was freezing in the cottage, yet she didn't even shiver. He knew from experience that wasn't a good thing.

"Let us warm you, shall we?" Her movements were stiff from the cold, and he didn't care for that. "I'll start a fire."

"No."

"Why?"

"I-I don't want him to f-find me."

He knelt before her, grasping her gloved hands in his. "No one will find us in this storm. You're safe now. I'll protect you."

When at last she nodded, he glanced at the empty woodbin. "I'll be back directly."

She nodded, her worried gaze following him out the door.

He found dry wood stacked under the overhang where he'd left his horse. In short order, he had a fire lit and slowly added more wood as the flames grew.

"Who is he?" Cole meant what he'd told her. He'd protect her. He berated himself for keeping his distance this past week. If he would've engaged with her, gotten to know her better, perhaps all this could've been avoided. He'd hadn't pressed her to tell him her secrets, as he had no desire to share his own.

She gave a trembling sigh but said nothing.

None of that mattered right now. He pulled her chair closer to the fire then removed her gloves so he could rub her hands. She gave no reaction to his movements. That was so unlike her. "Katherine?"

She only closed her eyes. Whether she didn't intend to tell him anything or was too cold, he didn't know.

Holding back his frustration, he reminded himself that she had no reason to trust him. Despite their kisses, he hadn't made much of an effort to befriend her.

Before worrying about any of that, he needed to warm her. He didn't know how long she'd been out in the cold. Frostbite could be setting in.

He drew her to her feet and removed her cloak as the fire burned brightly. "Forgive me for the impropriety of this, but we must warm you."

After removing his coat and hanging it on the other chair to dry, he sat and pulled her into his lap. With careful movements, he covered them with the blanket and her cloak. He wrapped his arms around her, hoping his body heat would help.

Katherine stared into the flames numbly. Within

a few minutes, she started to shiver. He took that as a good sign and rubbed her arms.

"He's my husband's b-brother."

The whispered words stopped him. He couldn't wrap his mind around the idea that Katherine was married. Disappointment crashed through him. She belonged to another. His thoughts flew to those two kisses. "You're married?"

"W-was. He passed away three years ago."

He wasn't proud of the relief that filled him but was grateful for the news all the same.

"What does he want?"

"To ruin whatever meager life I've pieced together."

Cole considered her words, reconciling them to his brief conversation with the man. "Why?"

"He blames me for Walter's death." Her head tipped down, hiding her expression.

Each piece of information she shared only raised more questions. None of this made sense. He wanted to demand she explain, but when she remained silent, he reminded himself to be patient.

What was important was that she was warm and comfortable. Then they could return to Crawford House. Perhaps he could enlist Grace's help to convince Katherine to talk. He glanced around, noting the pot hanging near the fire, and decided to find something with which to make a hot drink. That would help.

"I'll see if there's tea. If not, hot water might be the best I can manage." He slid her to the side and rose, tucking the makeshift blankets around her.

Within a short time, he'd fetched water from the well in back and had it steaming in the rinsed-out kettle. A search of the kitchen unveiled a tin of tea and cups.

She roused when he handed her the steaming cup, and her gaze finally met his. "Thank you, Cole."

He didn't care for what he saw in her eyes.

Defeat.

He recognized it, for he'd seen it several times in his own mirror. When the will to press on—to continue living—fell away.

"Katherine, I realize you don't know me, but I would help if I could." Her expression remained unchanged as she looked at him. He didn't think he was getting through to her. "I met him. He has a pocket watch with your picture in it."

Her eyes widened. "What did he say?"

"Only that he was searching for you." He moved her so once again, she sat on his lap. "I can't say that I cared for him."

She almost smiled at that. "Markus is very...determined. He loved his brother dearly and never cared for me." She turned to face him. "My name is Katherine Flemming. I don't wear glasses. And I'm a widow."

The way the words quickly tumbled out made him realize how much it had bothered her to lie.

She blinked back tears. "I'm tired of running and hiding. Why can't he understand that I'm sorry Walter died? I loved him too."

"What happened?"

"He fell ill with headaches and nausea. I wanted him to go to the doctor, but he insisted the apothecary knew more. Markus thinks I poisoned him." She looked at Cole again, her eyes pleading with him to understand. "I didn't. I never would've done something like that."

"I know." The sincerity in her expression and voice couldn't be denied. He believed her. It was that simple.

Regret and doubt flickered in those deep brown eyes.

"I-I should've done more. I should've made him see the doctor. I should've realized how ill he was. That the medicine was only making it worse."

"He was a grown man. How could you know his mind?"

Katherine only shook her head, obviously unable to forgive herself for what she hadn't done.

He knew that feeling as well. The same was true for him, as he had yet to forgive himself for the same reason.

When Katherine's tears fell, Cole took the cup from her hands to set it on the floor and pulled her tight into his embrace. "You're not to blame."

His whispered words only made her cry harder. Sobs shook her body. All he could think to do was hold her, whispering reassuring words that seemed to fall on deaf ears.

At last her tears subsided, and she drew a trembling breath. "I'm s-sorry."

"No apology is necessary. You've been through a terrible ordeal these past few years." He closed his eyes for a moment as he realized that was another experience they had in common. "You're entitled to tears."

"I've told him how sorry I am. That he can keep the money. But he doesn't care. When the police investigated and cleared me of any wrongdoing, it made no difference to him." She rested her head on his shoulder, snuggled into him in a way that made him ache and think of things that had no place here. "I left. I changed my name and took a position as a companion. But he found me and told the lady I worked for that I'd killed my husband and was hiding from the law. She dismissed me. I have changed names and positions more times than I can count."

"The last one being at the dressmaker's shop as Miss Flitchard."

"Yes. Where I met Grace. She's the first friend I've had in a long while."

Katherine might've been surrounded by people in the city, but it sounded as if she was as lonely as he. The notion had him tightening his arms around her. "I hope you consider me a friend as well."

He sensed her smile rather than saw it.

"I do, and I treasure it." She moved again, her forehead resting against his jaw.

The skin-to-skin contact made him heat from the inside out. Desire followed quickly on its heels, and his attention shifted to the feel of the woman in his arms. The sensations made him long for things that couldn't be, that he couldn't risk.

Despite that, his protective instincts flared to life. "I would help you with this, if you'd allow it. I can speak with him on your behalf."

"No." She sat up, eyes wide with alarm. "That will only make him more determined. Besides, I don't want him to know where I am. I would be horrified if he arrived at Crawford House. It would ruin Grace and Adair's Christmas, not to mention their guests'."

"Katherine—"

She placed a finger on his lips. "Thank you, but no. I'll decide on a course of action, but I need more time. I didn't think he'd find me so quickly."

He eased back and kissed her finger. "I hope you'll reconsider. My offer stands if you change your mind." He trailed a finger along her cheek. "You deserve to be happy, Katherine. But in order to do so, you might have to confront your past."

She tilted her head toward his caress. "I tried, but it did no good." She placed a hand on his to press it firmly to her cheek then closed her eyes as though enjoying his touch.

Temptation took hold, and he pressed his lips to hers. She startled, drawing back to look at him.

"Cole." The whispered name was filled with a myriad of emotions he couldn't identify, except one—longing.

That was all the invitation he needed. He captured her lips once more, the sweet taste of her heady, like fine brandy, and filling him with need.

His tongue danced with hers as her hand framed his face then shifted to tease the back of his neck.

Passion rose quickly, effortlessly. Whether it was the coziness of the cottage, or the response of the woman in his arms, he couldn't say, but he ached for her so badly that he could hardly breathe.

He tamped down his desire, telling himself the kisses were enough. But he wanted more. Katherine had seeped into him, slipping past his defenses. The idea of her leaving in a week was unbearable. Especially since she intended to disappear into a new identity.

He might have found her this time, but something told him he wouldn't the next.

The idea of that scared the hell out of him.

Chapter Eight

Katherine felt the intensity of Cole's kiss change. Deepen. The idea that this handsome man desired her was as intoxicating as the feel of him pressed close to her.

While she had no idea what her future might hold, she knew one thing—she wanted Cole. Here, now. If the past few years had taught her anything, it was to grab the few fleeting moments of happiness that crossed her path. They so rarely did.

But this—this was special. She recognized that undeniable fact with her heart and soul. Her feelings for this man had grown completely out of control while she'd been trying hard to ignore them.

It didn't escape her notice that he'd ridden all the way from Crawford House in the middle of a snowstorm to rescue her. How long had it been since anyone had cared enough to go to such measures for her?

Then he'd reassured her, built a fire, and made her tea. He was an honorable man, and she was better for having known him.

But as passion burned brighter between them, she knew it was all that and much more. She ran her fingers along the soft hair at the nape of his neck, gasping as he eased away only to press kisses along her neck.

"Oh, Cole," she muttered and tipped back her head, exposing her neck.

Their makeshift blankets slipped down, but Katherine was thoroughly heated now. Her fingers fumbled along his suit coat, undoing the buttons followed by the ones on his vest. She ran her hands along his linen shirt, loving the strength of his muscled form, from the cords of his broad shoulders to his chest then down along his ribs.

He might think her forward, but in this moment, she couldn't bring herself to care. As long as he didn't stop.

His kisses lowered to her neckline even as he ran his hands along her arm then her waist. When he moved his hand to tease the sensitive flesh at the top of her breasts, she moaned with pleasure.

"Katherine." It was both a plea and a demand.

She reveled that it was either. "Yes." She looked into his eyes, wanting him to understand her meaning. A crease marked the center of his brow. "Please."

As understanding came over his expression, she kissed him again and made her meaning clear. His tongue swirled with hers, sending waves of longing with each pass. She shifted on his lap, noting his erection against her hip.

Her movements left him breathless, and he broke the kiss. "I don't think you understand where this is leading."

"Cole." Again she met his gaze as she took his hand to press a kiss on the calloused palm. "I was married. I know exactly where this is going. I would be honored to make love with you."

Too late, she realized her word choice was all wrong. He hardly knew her. She couldn't expect him to feel anything for her other than simple desire. In this moment, that was enough. She held her breath, awaiting his answer.

"You offer too much," he protested.

"No. I *want* too much." Disappointment flowed through her at his hesitation. "Let us offer comfort to each other, however briefly. When the holiday is over, I must leave, and you must return to your life. Why not enjoy these stolen moments?"

"You tempt me, Katherine." He swallowed hard. "You have no idea what you do to me."

"Then show me. Please." Made bold by the heat in his hazel eyes, she pressed his hand to her breast.

Holding her gaze, he molded it with his fingers then reached behind her to loosen her bodice. He continued to caress her as she quickly shed it. She rose and stood before the fire as she removed her gown, leaving her in her corset and chemise.

The admiration on his face as he watched her made desire pool low in her belly. As she untied the ribbons of her corset, he stood. "May I assist you?"

"Oh, yes," she responded with a smile.

Soon the corset rested on top of her gown. He reached out a finger to touch the tip of her breast, causing her to jolt in reaction. He caressed the mound, and her breath came faster. Then he bent to take her nipple into his mouth, chemise and all.

She caught her breath as he touched her other breast. When he drew the chemise down to take her nipple into his mouth, she closed her eyes with the pleasure. He kissed her again, sending her head spinning as her body grew languid with desire.

She slid her hands over his shoulders, removing his coat and vest in one movement. She dearly wanted to see what he looked like underneath all those clothes. With quick fingers, she undid his shirt and allowed it to drop to the floor as she took in the sight before her.

"My goodness." She ran her hands along his torso, loving the feel of his muscles, the coarse hair of his chest, how it tapered to a narrow line leading lower.

The sweetness of the moment struck her—snow falling outside, a fire blazing inside, but most of all, the man before her. It was her fairytale come to life.

"It's perfect here. You're perfect." She rose up on her toes to kiss him again, loving the feel of him against her scantily clad form.

"I want to see you, Katherine. All of you." He tugged the ribbon of her chemise and removed the garment in quick order.

She stood bare before him, resisting the urge to shield her flaws as his gaze swept over her.

"So beautiful," he murmured, then took her into his arms. The heat of his body set hers on fire. "So perfect."

Within moments, he'd shed his trousers, groaning when she caressed his shaft. He took her hand and held it as he caught his breath. "Are you certain?"

"Completely."

He sat on the chair and drew her onto his lap, facing him, one knee on either side of his legs. As he kissed her deeply, his hands roamed everywhere, heating her until she could stand it no more.

His hand trailed up her bare thigh to the sensitive skin of her hip then to the apex of her thighs, brushing against her damp curls. When his finger touched her very center, her thighs tightened in reaction. His movements drove her higher, and it was all she could do not to cry out.

"Now," she begged.

"Yes." He lifted her hips to ease himself inside her, slowly, inch by glorious inch.

The sensation of being one with this man was overwhelming, bringing tears to her eyes as desire built, layer upon layer. He held her hips, lifting her time and again in a rhythm as old as life itself.

When she thought she could bear no more, he reached between them, stroking her moist folds, sending her flying high to break into a million pieces. Then his body pulsed with his own release.

As this strong man held her so gently and her body floated back to earth, Katherine could only sigh with delight at the unexpected turn life had taken.

She didn't want to think of her past or the days to come—only this moment.

Perhaps Christmas held some magic after all.

Chapter Nine

Cole stared out across the moonlit, snow-covered fields through the ballroom window the next evening. The Christmas ball would begin within the hour. From what he could tell, Adair and Grace had invited half the countryside.

But it was the lovely interlude with Katherine at the cottage that held his thoughts.

When the snow had slowed as dusk approached, Cole had taken the chance of returning to Crawford House before dark fell. Though loath to leave the intimacy of the cottage, it wasn't practical to stay. Not when they had no food, and everyone at Crawford House was worried about Katherine.

Despite her insistence that he not confront Markus, Cole dearly wanted to. As ridiculous as it was, he wanted to save her, to give her back her life. And if the possibility of seeing her again crossed his mind, who would blame him? After all, there was a chance she might be expecting a child. Never mind that she'd dismissed his concerns because she hadn't conceived a child with her husband.

Somewhere in the past ten days, Katherine had given him a glimpse of what life could be like. While he was safer keeping his distance from others, he now realized his isolation made for a miserable existence. Avoiding pain meant avoiding happiness. Could he truly live the rest of his life doing that?

He eyed the kissing bough hanging just to the left of where he stood in a private alcove. With careful planning, he intended to make sure he and Katherine danced beneath it. He couldn't wait to hold her again. He wanted to make her see they had something special, despite—or maybe because of—their pasts.

He wasn't sure what to call these growing feelings he had for her, and he wasn't about to let her go until he found out. The future was uncertain, but he wanted to explore what they had together, as he knew it was special.

Could he find a way to convince her to agree?

Katherine smoothed the gown Grace had insisted she wear for the ball. The pale blue and lace design made her feel like an ice princess. It was far too elegant and would draw too much attention. Yet she couldn't help but wonder what Cole would think of it.

The maid had already been by to curl her hair into long ringlets that fell down her back.

In truth, Katherine hardly recognized the woman in the mirror.

A knock on her door signaled Grace's arrival.

"Oh." Grace paused in the doorway as she took in Katherine's appearance.

"It's too much. The neckline—"

"Shows your generous curves."

Katherine frowned. That wasn't what she'd meant at all. "The waist is far too—"

"It's perfect. I knew it would be." Grace moved into the room to take Katherine's hands in hers. "You look beautiful."

Katherine shook her head but couldn't hold back her smile. "You look amazing."

Grace's gown was a rich red trimmed with white satin. With a grin, she released Katherine's hands and spun in a circle. "We look wonderful, don't we?"

"We do." Katherine attempted to set aside her unease.

The hours after the incredible afternoon in the cottage with Cole had been a blur. They hadn't had any time alone together, but the heated glances they'd shared across the dinner table made her heart flutter and her stomach dance.

The numerous times she reminded herself that she'd be leaving Cole and this fairytale for a new identity in a few short days didn't stop the flutters or the dancing.

She refused to worry about any of that tonight. Christmas would be here in two days, and she hoped to stay until then. Somehow she needed to set aside her concern and enjoy this brief respite.

"Will you be dancing with Cole this evening?" Grace asked, dark eyes sparkling.

"I dearly hope so." Katherine hesitated, holding Grace's hand a moment longer, gaining her friend's attention.

"What is it?"

"There's something I want to tell you, that I've wanted to share with you for a long while." She swallowed hard, wanting desperately to tell Grace everything, that she wasn't who Grace thought she was.

The brisk knock on the door took both of them by surprise.

"Come in," Grace called out.

Adair peeked in. "Our guests are arriving. Are you two lovely ladies ready?"

Grace turned back to Katherine with brow raised.

"Of course." Katherine knew the opportunity was lost. She would find another to explain to Grace about the lies she'd told and ask for forgiveness. It had waited this long. A little longer wouldn't hurt.

Katherine left the handsome couple in the foyer to greet their guests and entered the ballroom, intending to make one last circuit around the room to ensure all was as it should be.

She couldn't help but stop to admire the room. It truly was perfect. The refreshment table was set up just as Grace wanted, complete with small Christmas cakes and biscuits baked by the cook this morning, along with an enormous bowl of wassail punch. More substantial fare would be served in a side room as the evening progressed. The musicians were warming up at the far end. Footmen would mingle amid the guests with trays of drinks and cakes.

"Good evening."

The deep voice sent awareness spearing through her, for she knew exactly to whom it belonged. Unwelcome tears stung her eyes. She blinked quickly, reminding herself this night would warm her in the nights to come. She wasn't about to ruin it by becoming overly emotional.

Forcing a smile, she turned to face Cole, her heart doing a long, slow roll at the sight of him. Her smile grew as she took in his appearance. "You look so handsome."

He frowned at her comment, making her grin. "I believe the compliment should be for me to say." His gaze swept up and down her form, his expression softening. He took her hand in his and lifted it to his lips. "You are beautiful."

The intensity of his gaze caught her breath. It almost allowed her to forget who she was. "Thank you, my lord."

"May I have the honor of a dance or two?"

"I would enjoy that more than anything."

He tucked her hand under his elbow as though he never intended to let her go, then turned so they could face the entrance.

The night was already going beyond her wildest dreams. She closed her eyes, trying to press the moment on her heart to remember forever. She couldn't allow the emotion welling up inside her to ruin everything.

Cole's happiness lifted her mood. He was charming as he told her who was who amidst the local lords and ladies arriving. His insightful comments showed how much he cared about the people who lived here. His connection to his community was impressive and heartwarming, but unfamiliar to her. She'd never had those sort of ties.

At last Grace and Adair joined the growing crowd in the ballroom and the ball began in earnest.

"Shall we?" Cole asked.

Her heart soaring, Katherine walked with him to the dance floor, hoping she remembered the proper steps. It had been a long time since she'd danced.

Waltzing with Cole was as close to flying as she could imagine. She felt so graceful in his arms, and his attentiveness set her heart pounding.

A commotion rippled through the crowd, causing the dancers on the floor to halt.

"What—" Her question didn't fully form as she saw who stood near Grace and Adair only a few feet away.

Markus.

Panic choked her. Every instinct in her body screamed for her to run.

Yet the feel of Cole's arm around her anchored her. As she hesitated between standing to fight and running once again to avoid the terrible accusations she knew Markus would utter, Grace turned to look at her. Her expression of confusion, doubt, and hurt twisted Katherine's heart.

Why hadn't she told her friend the truth weeks ago?

Adair's expression had cooled. Obviously Markus had already said much of what he came to say. "Perhaps you should explain, Mrs. Flemming."

Katherine's mind went blank, unable to think of what to say. Once again, her world was falling apart. She turned to Cole, fearful of what he might think.

All she saw was patient understanding as he met her gaze. "Tell them the truth," he urged.

"Katherine, what is all this about?" Grace asked.

"Yes, tell them," Markus insisted. "Explain how you murdered your husband, my brother. How you poisoned him so you could have his money."

"No! It wasn't like that." Katherine looked at her friends, desperate to make them believe her but holding no hope they would. The guests gathered around them, making her want to flee. Fear and remorse choked her.

Cole brought her closer to his side as though lending her his strength. He nodded encouragement. "Continue."

"Don't listen to anything this murderess has to say. She killed my brother."

She ignored the gasp of the crowd, keeping her focus on Cole's presence. She'd never had anyone at her side when Markus had confronted her in the past. It was a novel experience that gave her the will to try to make Markus listen to reason.

"I begged him to let me send for the doctor. But he insisted the medicine the apothecary prescribed was helping." She tapped the corner of her eye. "I tried to stop him. His ring caught me when we struggled over it."

Markus glanced at her scar even as his lips tightened. "It contained poison, and you knew it. That's why you gave it to him morning and night."

"You are right," she agreed, surprising Markus. "I have spoken with doctors who confirmed two of the ingredients were poisonous. Perhaps harmless in smaller doses. But the apothecary mistakenly told Walter to take it more often than he should've."

She turned to Cole, then to Grace and Adair, doing her best to ignore everyone else. "I loved my husband. He was a good man. I didn't want him to die, let alone suffer."

Cole took her hand and squeezed it tight. "I don't believe for a moment that you would deliberately harm another."

The shadows in Cole's eyes that had lightened in the past few days returned as he looked at Markus. "I understand how you feel, what it's like to be the only one left behind, the sole survivor. You see, I lost my mother, father, and sister two years ago to influenza. I was gone, traveling, enjoying adventures with friends while they were ill." He looked away, his pain palpable. "I wish I had been there. Maybe I could've done something to save them. I think of that every day. The guilt is unbearable at times."

Katherine's heart tugged at his distress. That explained so much.

Markus scowled. "Someone should pay for my brother's untimely death."

Katherine's heart sank. Would this nightmare never end? What more could she say to make him understand?

"I felt the same way," Cole said. "I chose to blame myself."

"I'm sorry, Markus," Katherine offered, unwilling to give up. "Sorrier than you'll ever know. I should've done more." She closed her eyes. "I should've made him listen."

"He was so stubborn." Markus caught her gaze when she opened her eyes, the anger in his expression shifting to reveal his grief. "He rarely listened to me either."

"Sometimes bad things—terrible things—happen," Cole said. "It's no one's fault." He looked at Katherine. "And sometimes good things happen when you least expect them."

Katherine felt her heart swell. Cole's unwavering support meant the world to her. "I don't want the money, Markus. I never wanted it. It is yours."

Adair cleared his throat. "Mr. Flemming, I hope you find Katherine's explanation satisfactory. We certainly do." His tone held all the nobility of his title. "She is a dear friend of ours."

Cole squeezed Katherine's hand again. "We hold her in the highest regard."

Markus glanced around, as though finally noting the crowd gathered around them. "I suppose

I allowed my grief to turn into something else. I wanted someone to be punished. My apologies for interrupting your celebration." He turned to face Katherine. "I was convinced you married Walter for the money."

"I never wanted it. You should keep it as it belongs to the family, not me." Katherine wanted no part of the money. Not after all that had occurred.

Markus cleared his throat. "I'm sorry, Katherine."

A sob caught in her throat. His apology was something she'd never expected. The idea of having her life back made her legs tremble. "So am I. Walter was a good man."

Grace hooked her arm through Katherine's, her smile filling Katherine with relief. "You are welcome to join us, sir."

"At least have a cup of wassail. It's cold out this evening." Cole raised a brow at Katherine as though to make certain she agreed.

"Do stay, Markus. Christmas shouldn't be spent alone." She shared a long look with Cole, hoping he truly heard her. They'd both spent too much time alone. This Christmas would be different.

"I couldn't," Markus protested.

It took Adair's insistence, but soon Markus held a cup in one hand and a Christmas cake in the other and was visiting with a local squire.

"Is it really over? After all these years?" She stared at Markus in disbelief, blinking back tears.

"The support of friends can change everything." Cole's deep voice sent shivers down her back. "It helps us forgive ourselves for the past. That is something we both need to work on." He turned to face her. "Where were we?"

"I believe we were dancing."

With a smile, he swept her into another waltz. But within moments, he eased into a small alcove and stopped to look up.

She followed his gaze and saw the kissing bough above her. "Oh, my."

"Exactly." He kissed her, gently yet thoroughly, setting her soul singing with joy.

"Don't forget to pluck a berry from the bough," she said with a smile.

He did as she suggested and held it high. "I'm keeping this for good luck."

Katherine leaned back to look into his eyes. "I'm so sorry for your loss. I can't imagine what you've been through."

"I miss them every day. I was doing all I could to avoid the future."

"And I've been doing all I can to escape my past. We're quite the pair."

"You've changed all that for me, Katherine." He reached out to touch her cheek, and her heart swelled. With love.

Her eyes widened at the realization. *Love?* That wasn't possible. Not yet. Was it?

"I know we haven't known each other long," Cole said, his voice quiet, "but I love you. Every Christmas, I want to dance under the mistletoe with you for as many years as we can possibly have together.

Will you marry me?"

Blinking back tears, Katherine wrapped her arms around him as she rose on her toes to kiss him. "Yes. And we will enjoy each day in between all the Christmases, shall we?"

"You never know what might happen when you dance under the mistletoe."

"It holds a special magic, doesn't it?"

"Along with love."

What could she do but kiss him again?

Epilogue

London, England, April 1871

Cole tapped his toe to the swell of the music, surprised to realize he was enjoying himself—at a London ball no less. But when a life was as happy as his was, what could one do but enjoy the moment?

They had rented a townhome in Mayfair, not far from Grace and Adair's. It had taken some talking on Grace's part to convince Katherine to agree to attend the London Season. Now that they were here, they were having a marvelous time. Katherine knew London well but the events they'd attended thus far had been completely different than anything she'd done in her previous life.

He glanced at his beautiful wife, hiding a smile even as Katherine tried to cover her yawn. Her tiredness was only one of the symptoms she was displaying. How much more time would pass before she realized she was expecting? She'd been so certain she was barren since she'd been married for several years without conceiving. He supposed it had never occurred to her that the fault lay with her previous husband, not her.

"Good evening." Captain Hawke and his wife joined them, along with Viscount Frost and his wife. "Is my brother here?" Hawke asked.

"I haven't seen him yet," Cole responded.

"I can't believe another Season is upon us." Viscountess Frost smiled as she looked over the crowd. "Quite a few debutantes."

"Poor things," Mrs. Hawke commented, only to be nudged in the side by the viscountess.

"Come now, Lettie. Don't you remember the excitement of your first Season?"

"No. I can't say that I do."

Captain Hawke drew her gloved hand to his lips to kiss her knuckles. "I don't know about the rest of you, but I for one am pleased those days are behind us. I'm right where I want to be, and I wouldn't trade it for the world."

Katherine turned to Cole. "I would have to agree, wouldn't you?" Her smile lit her face. "The past four months have changed my life beyond anything I could've dreamed."

The happiness in his heart grew brighter at her words. He longed to draw her into his arms and show her how much he agreed. But that would have to wait until they were alone. "I couldn't agree more."

"Katherine," Julia said as she studied her, "you're positively glowing this evening."

Katherine blinked in surprise. "I suppose it's because I'm so happy. All this is new to me, so it's like my first Season."

Cole couldn't help his smug smile, well aware that happiness wasn't the only reason she was glowing. The captain caught his gaze, his eyes narrowing as though he might've guessed Cole's thoughts. That only made Cole smile all the more. He couldn't wait until they could share the news with their new friends.

"Lettie, will your sisters be here this evening?" Frost asked, looking about as though searching for them.

"I believe so. Mother doesn't miss any of the major balls unless there's a natural disaster that prevents her from attending. Why?"

"It was the oddest thing, but I swear I saw Daphne in Whitechapel today," Frost said with a shake of his head.

"Why were you in Whitechapel?" Cole asked. "That area of London is not for the faint of heart."

"We like to keep an eye on a few areas and monitor activity," Hawke responded.

"If you'd truly like to know why they roam through Whitechapel and some of the other poorer neighborhoods, I'd be happy to give you a book called *The Seven Curses of London*," Mrs. Hawke offered. "It's difficult to read of the problems the city faces, but I'm proud to say we've made some small progress."

Hawke smiled at his wife then turned to Cole. "We have indeed. But from what we've learned lately, more trouble is brewing, hence the reason Frost was in the area today."

"I'd like to learn more of these curses," Cole said. "Problems that plague London often ease into the country. It would make sense to attempt to do what we can here, before the problems worsen and spread."

"We'll send over a copy of the book," Mrs. Hawke offered then turned to Frost. "You must've been mistaken about Daphne. There's no reason she would've been in that area. When I've mentioned the *Seven Curses* in the past, she merely rolled her eyes at me."

Frost nodded. "I'm sure you're right."

Mrs. Hawke scowled. "All the same, I'll speak with her to see if anything is afoot. She manages to find trouble where no one else does."

The notes of the beginning of a waltz filled the air, causing Cole to turn to Katherine. "May I have the honor of this dance?"

"I'd love to," she agreed with a smile.

After excusing themselves from the others, they moved to the dance floor, and Cole took her into his arms. "I'll never grow weary of dancing with you."

"I feel the same." She smiled then glanced around the other dancers. "I am still growing accustomed to not having to watch over my shoulder every time we're out."

"I am adjusting to the changes in my life as well," Cole said. "Being this happy every day takes getting used to."

Katherine chuckled. "I agree." She started to yawn again. "I am terribly sorry. I don't know why

I'm so tired of late."

Cole waited, watching her to see if she pieced the clues together. To his delight, realization came slowly over her face, followed by a hint of panic.

"Cole?" Her tone was higher than normal.

"Yes, my love." He swung her across the floor, tamping down the urge to do a quick jig.

"I believe I have some news to share."

"Yes, you do."

Her gaze tangled with his as her breath hitched. "You already know?"

"I suspected."

"Cole, we are going to have a baby," she whispered. Her eyes flooded with tears, and her breath hitched again.

"Yes, we're going to have a baby."

Her face crumpled at his words.

Heart clenching, he quickly eased them to a terrace door so they could step outside to the garden for a moment of privacy. "Why are you crying?" he asked as he pulled her into his arms.

"Because I'm so happy," she managed between sobs.

Relief filled him. "I am delighted as well." He kissed her gently then held her, giving them both time to adjust to the idea of a babe.

She leaned back to look into his eyes. "You're certain you want this?"

"Absolutely." He placed a hand on the soft swell of her stomach. "We're going to be excellent parents."

She placed her hand over his. The brightness of her smile erased the evidence of her tears. "Yes, we are." She lifted up on her toes as she wrapped her arms around him and kissed him. "To think all this started with some mistletoe."

"We need to make certain we have it in our home every year. Apparently, it brings us luck, for it brought me you." Cole kissed Katherine as they swayed to the music in their hearts.

The End

~*~

Here's a preview of TEMPTING THE SCOUNDREL, the next story in The Seven Curses of London series, available now.

Chapter One

London, April 1871

Elliott Walker, the Earl of Aberland, gave a sigh of relief as the hansom cab drew to a halt before his Mayfair residence. He paused after alighting, his gaze taking in the impressive entrance with its white fluted pillars and marble steps that he was fortunate enough to call home.

Each trip abroad made him more grateful to return to the peace he found within its walls. His secret position with the British Intelligence Office forced him to travel far more than he preferred.

This last visit to the Continent had been especially trying, causing him to question how much longer he wanted to continue. Playing the role of scoundrel to gather intelligence had become exhausting, and he was weary to the bone.

For the moment, he intended to put all his questions and doubts aside and enjoy time at home. The house was filled with pleasant memories, but even better, his beloved grandmother resided here. He smiled in anticipation of seeing her.

The door opened and two liveried footmen hurried out, greeting him with a bow before tending to his bags.

Codwell, his longtime butler, waited by the door, smiling broadly as Elliott walked up the steps. "Welcome home, my lord."

"Thank you, Codwell. I trust all has been well in my absence?"

"Indeed."

If it weren't for his special training and natural instincts, Elliott might have missed the hesitancy in Codwell's manner. His thoughts flew to his grandmother. "Is all well with the countess?"

"Yes. She is most anxious to see you."

Guilt speared through Elliott. He'd been gone nearly four weeks, leaving his grandmother alone. He had the utmost faith in Codwell and the rest of the staff to keep watch over her safety, but she needed more than that. "I hope she's enjoying the beginning of the Season."

"Actually, I'd venture to say she's reveling in it."

"Oh?" Elliott stepped into the foyer, glancing about as though he might spot what caused his unease. Codwell's words sank in, returning his focus to the older man who'd been with his family since he was a young boy. "Reveling, you say?"

That wasn't like his grandmother. While she normally enjoyed attending a few events, he wouldn't have described her participation in previous years as "reveling."

The butler cleared his throat, shifting away his gaze briefly. "We have a new addition to the household."

"Who would that be?" Anger slid into Elliott, tightening his chest. Codwell knew a few details of Elliott's double life, so he understood why this news would not be welcome.

"With your long absence, your uncle feared the countess might be lonely, so he hired a companion for her, a Miss Sophia Markham."

The footmen entered with his bags, forcing Elliott to wait to have his questions answered. And he had many. While he detested the idea of his grandmother being lonely, he equally detested the idea of a stranger living in his house.

He imagined a nosy, elderly spinster who refused to mind her own business. The idea of the sanctuary of his home breached by a stranger was impossible. He took care to hide his activities from the staff, with the exception of the butler and his grandmother, but he had no desire to evade another set of watchful eyes.

No. It simply wasn't bearable.

The butler turned to direct the footmen to take care with his belongings, and Elliott opened the door of his library only to stop short, startled to find a woman there, perusing the bookshelves. *His* bookshelves.

As though feeling the weight of his regard, the young lady turned to face him, her eyes widening in surprise. Lovely hazel eyes set in an attractive face. But none of that mattered. She was in *his* library, the one place he depended on as his refuge.

"My lord, may I introduce Miss Sophia Markham, your grandmother's new companion?" Codwell asked.

No, you may not. He bit his tongue to keep the words from slipping out, yet he saw nothing but complications when he looked at this woman.

Where was the elderly spinster who would be better suited for his grandmother? This young lady was the very opposite of what he'd expected. Dark curls framed her face, as though refusing to be tamed. Her alabaster skin begged to be touched, and one dark brow rose, as if already questioning him.

"Good day." He knew his tone was churlish and less than polite but couldn't seem to help himself.

She opened her mouth to respond then quickly closed it, instead dipping into a low curtsy. "My lord."

The surprise in her expression at his presence gave him a small measure of satisfaction. Perhaps he wasn't the only one feeling off balance.

He scowled. Why did she have to be so lovely? He would've much preferred the aging spinster he'd imagined.

She rose from her graceful curtsy in her plain grey gown and clasped her hands before her. "I'm terribly sorry to intrude in your library." Did she have the ability to read minds? "I was searching for a new book to read to the countess."

A likely story. His gaze swung toward his desk. But of course the polished mahogany was empty except for his grandfather's gold clock on its gleaming surface. He hadn't left any clues for an inquisitive guest to find, nor had any arrived in his absence.

The idea of having to guard against a nosy stranger who made herself at home in his library made him even wearier. He couldn't do it. Not only did his grandmother reside in his house, he spent a significant amount of time with her when he was home. That meant he'd be in contact with this young lady frequently. Far too frequently.

But before he did anything rash, such as send her packing, he would speak with his grandmother. If this woman was here at his uncle's behest, surely his grandmother wouldn't miss her company. Elliott would be rid of her in no time.

"I hope you found something of interest," he said at last.

She turned to pluck a slim leather-bound volume from a shelf. "This will do until the books we ordered arrive."

"What books would those be?" He was curious as to what his grandmother had been up to in his absence.

"*The Mystery of Edwin Drood* by Charles Dickens and *The Seven Curses of London* by James Greenwood." She lifted her chin, as though expecting him to question the choices. "Have you read either?"

"I can't say I have. *The Seven Curses*?"

"I understand the author shares the seven worst problems plaguing the city."

While his grandmother often read fiction, since when had she become interested in social issues?

He'd obviously been gone far too long.

Miss Markham pursed her lips. "Perhaps you might enjoy learning more about such problems."

He sighed at the hint of disapproval in her expression. His reputation had preceded him. While he knew he should be pleased his cover as a philandering rogue was secure, he'd grown weary of it.

"I shall rely on your report of it." He gave his signature careless smile as he moved closer, which only had her tightening her lips further.

Her unfavorable opinion of him could prove useful. Perhaps getting rid of her would be easier than he expected.

TEMPTING THE SCOUNDREL, a novella, is available now.

Other Books By Lana Williams

Victorian Romances

The Seven Curses of London Series:

Trusting the Wolfe, a Novella, Book .5
Loving the Hawke, Book I
Charming the Scholar, Book II
Rescuing the Earl, Book III
Dancing Under the Mistletoe, a Christmas Novella, Book IV
Tempting the Scoundrel, a Novella, Book V
   Romancing the Rogue, a Regency Prequel
Falling For the Viscount, Book VI
Daring the Duke, Book VII
Wishing Upon A Christmas Star, a Novella
Ruby's Gamble, a Novella
Gambling for the Governess, Book IX
Redeeming the Lady, Book X

The Secret Trilogy:

Unraveling Secrets, Book I
Passionate Secrets, Book II

Shattered Secrets, Book III

Regency Romances

The Rogue Chronicles:

Romancing the Rogue, Book 1

A Rogue's Reputation, a Christmas Novella, Book 2

A Rogue No More, Book 3

A Rogue to the Rescue, Book 4

A Rogue and Some Mistletoe, Book 5

A Match Made in the Highlands, a Novella

Medieval Romances:

Falling for A Knight Series:

A Knight's Christmas Wish, Novella, Book .5

A Knight's Quest, Book 1

A Knight's Temptation, Book 2

A Knight's Captive, Book 3

The Vengeance Trilogy:

A Vow To Keep, Book I

A Knight's Kiss, Novella, Book 1.5

Trust In Me, Book II

Believe In Me, Book III

Contemporary Romances:

Yours for the Weekend, a Novella

Reviews help readers and authors, and I'd be honored if you'd write one, no matter how brief!

About the Author

Lana Williams is a USA Today Bestselling Author who writes historical romance filled with mystery, adventure, and a pinch of paranormal to stir things up. Filled with a love of books from an early age, Lana put pen to paper and decided happy endings were a must in any story she created.

Her latest series is The Seven Curses of London, set in Victorian times, and shares stories of men and women who attempt to battle the ills of London, and the love they find along the way that truly gives them something worth fighting for.

The Rogue Chronicles - where rogues meet their match in the most delightful way - are set in Regency London and begin with Romancing the Rogue.

Her first medieval trilogy is set in England and follows heroes seeking vengeance only to find love when they least expect it. The second trilogy begins on the Scottish border and follows the second generation of the de Bremont family.

The Secret Trilogy, which shares stories set in Victorian London, follows three lords injured in an electromagnetic experiment that went terribly wrong and the women who help heal them through the power of love.

She writes in the Rocky Mountains with her husband, two growing sons, and two labs, and loves hearing from readers. Stop by her website and say hello at www.lanawilliams.net.